Hailing from Govan, Glasgow, the author was a primary school head teacher for a number of years. Retiring early, he took up writing and *Hadrian and the Moonbiscuit* was born.

HADRIAN
AND THE
MOONBISCUIT

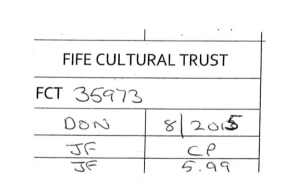

I dedicate this novel to my wonderful wife Linda and to my incredible daughter Julie, for their constant love, support and encouragement.

Andrew Kilgariff

HADRIAN AND THE MOONBISCUIT

AUSTIN & MACAULEY
PUBLISHERS LTD.

A CIP catalogue record for this title is
available from the British Library.

ISBN 978 1 84963 219 5

www.austinmacauley.com

First Published (2013)
Austin & Macauley Publishers Ltd.
25 Canada Square
Canary Wharf
London
E14 5LB

Printed & Bound in Great Britain

CONTENTS

CHAPTER ZERO

Hadrian Wall is eleven years old. He is an only child. He lives in a modern estate near to his school. Hadrian would do better at school if he paid more attention, but finds it hard to concentrate when he's bored. He seems to be good at writing, problem-solving, sport and maths.

Hadrian has a host of games for his PlayStation and spends much of his free time enjoying them. He also plays chess and football – in both cases for his school – and likes swimming and playing with friends. His best friend is Robbie Romans. Robbie has a sister Lorna, who is twelve and drop dead gorgeous. Hadrian has a very strong but *very* secret crush on her.

He doesn't have a favourite food, but is pleased when he gets chicken, chips, pizza, Chinese food, grated raw carrot, most fruit and all chocolate. He hates Brussels sprouts, mushrooms and butter beans.

He enjoys wearing jeans, white trainers, hoodies and T-shirts and is very uncomfortable in school uniform, except the sweatshirts and especially the tie.

He will be twelve soon and would dearly like a mountain bike like Robbie's for his birthday.

Hadrian has never been to the moon before.

CHAPTER 1

Hadrian's eyes sprang open. Why had he wakened up so suddenly in the middle of the night? He lay flat on his back while his eyes pierced the darkness for a clue. It was pitch black darkness. Not a chink of light peeped in anywhere in his bedroom. His heart thudded in his ears. He felt beads of sweat forming on his temple and on his top lip. He wanted to lick his lips, but couldn't. He wanted to shout, "Who's there?"

Slowly, extremely slowly, he drew his right hand out from under the duvet and ran his fingers quietly over his eyelashes to check that his eyes were open. A rasping sound started up very near the bed and Hadrian's pulse accelerated. He wanted to shout out to his dad and mum, but his throat seemed to be closed. He suddenly realised that the rasping sound was his own breathing. Something had wakened him, though. He strained every one of his five senses to try and identify any other presence in the room. Although there was nothing to be seen, heard, touched, smelled or tasted, he was still unsettled.

Hadrian normally felt a bit miffed when his mother popped her head round the door on her way to bed. What eleven-year-old wanted to be tucked in and have a kiss planted on his forehead by his mother? How he wished she would pop her head in right now! How he would welcome the light being on and a friendly face bending over his bed. His eyes were beginning to adapt to the dark and he could vaguely make out a slightly less dense rectangle over on the other side of the room. The curtains! Could he get safely over to them without whoever was in the room getting him? Hadrian thought of switching on the bedside lamp but dismissed that idea right away. Light would mean that he could be seen just as easily by any intruder as he would be able to see it. Was it a burglar? He had to do something! Now! In a split second he had rolled off his bed onto the floor on the side further away from the window. As soon as he made contact with the floor, he spun over and rolled underneath his bed, emerging nearer to the curtains. Pausing only to scramble into a sprint start crouched position, he launched himself in the direction of the window. Hadrian clawed at the heavy curtains and yanked them open in one swift movement. Moonlight flooded the area from window to bed and immediate surrounds. There was no-one in that area. He peered into the faraway darkest corner of his room and croaked unconvincingly; "I see you. I know you're there!"

While speaking, he lifted his cricket bat from its

leaning position by the window. He crept towards his bed, swishing the bat slowly and widely round his head. He flicked on the bedside lamp. Gooseflesh spread over his back, arms and legs as he stared at his empty room. He almost sobbed with relief. God! He had never been so frightened in his life. He still felt slightly nauseous and uneasy, even though he could see there was no one there. He walked to his window and replaced the bat. He surveyed the street scene below. There was nothing unusual down there; a couple of cats were mooching about as a polythene bag skipped up the road on the breeze. The pavements were basking in the soft sodium glow of the street lights. The sound of a tired car, a few blocks away, lent a soft purr to the peaceful setting below.

Hadrian allowed himself the luxury of a huge stretch and yawn and was about to return to bed when: WHOOSH! WHEEEE! *ZZZZZSWIZZZZ*, "What the hell was that?!" gasped Hadrian. His curtains billowed up like paper tissues, flapping wildly about in a fully-stretched horizontal position at the ceiling. His windows rattled like two dice in a cup. A brief chill cut through Hadrian like a dagger and his bedside light flickered madly. Then, as quickly as it had happened, it stopped. Hadrian spun round and gave a yelp of fear and disbelief. There, by his bed, was something that had to be from outer space. He gawped at it for fully two minutes, while it just stood there – if 'stood' was the right word – as it had a sphere the shape of a size 5 football as its 'feet'. Hadrian looked it over from top to bottom and had the distinct impression it was doing the same to him. Its one eye was on a sort of miniature elephant trunk emerging from the middle of what must have been its face. While Hadrian cast his gaze over the creature, its eye was twisting and turning in every direction, absorbing him. What on earth was it? How did it get into his room without breaking the window or making a hole in the wall? His bedroom door was still shut and had no sign of any damage. This was very, very, strange. Still this thing stayed where it was, making no noise whatsoever. Hadrian was having an internal struggle between fear and intrigue. The longer the two beings looked warily at each other, the more the fear diminished inside Hadrian. It reached the point when he thought he was feeling more curiosity than fear, perhaps because this creature was not very tall. It was only up to his shoulders. His heart was still bumping, however, as there was still *some* fear. What an odd head it had. It reminded Hadrian of an apple when someone had nibbled all the way round it, leaving the top and bottom untouched but the middle bitten in right to the seed compartments. The chameleon-type eye was spooky and there was just a mesh grille where a human mouth would be. Its entire skin was like elephant hide with two diagonal flaps across its lower 'chest'. As for arms, well two grew from its right shoulder and one from its left. This latter one was like a long skinny human arm and ended in a paddle, rather than a hand.

The paddle had a grille on it like the one on its face. Hadrian was to find out later that this space boy from Jupiter had to cover the 'mouth' with the paddle in order to communicate. The outer right arm was thick, about 70cms long and had powerful-looking pincers at the end. The inner arm was much thinner and ended in four prongs, the outer two being curved and the inners shorter, straight and sharp. The arm seemed to be moving in and out as Hadrian examined it, as if it could extend considerably. Having no legs, the torso tapered onto the sphere which rotated in small circles continuously while the creature remained in the one position. It was like watching a mono cyclist from Mars. "Wh-what are you?" Hadrian ventured.

The creature clamped its mesh paw over its facial grille. Sounds like rapid machine-gun fire came from the creature's mesh mouth. While this harsh sound was rattling from it, the monster used the thin arm from its right side to rummage in one of the flaps in its torso. Having taken a small luminous disc from the flap, the creature's arm extended slowly towards Hadrian's face with the disc, while continuing to produce the machine-gun noise. Hadrian didn't know whether to move, or shout or hit the arm away. In the end he did nothing. The arm slowly approached his forehead with the disc. Was he about to be put under a spell? Was he being captured by aliens? Would he turn into one of the space invaders? Was this thing going to suck out his brains? He decided not to wait to find out and to run out of his room and fetch his parents. His body did not respond. He tried to call for help as the disc almost touched him. No sound escaped and the disc pressed cool against his trembling brow. The arm retracted much more quickly than it had approached him. He could feel something cold on his forehead and reached up to explore it with his right hand. His hand couldn't locate anything, but he could feel that something had happened to his forehead. What had this thing done to him? At this point he became really frightened for his future. He was about to panic.

The rapid clicking sounds emanated from the space creature once again. This time however, although Hadrian could clearly hear the rapid clicks coming from the grille covered by the paddle, inside his head he heard; "By dabe iz Greeorr."

Hadrian tingled in every nerve. This thing on his head meant he could hear its speech. Was it trying to tell him its name? "By dname izz Greeor," it repeated.

"My name is Hadrian," he managed a hoarse whisper and waited to see if he had been correct. "Did you say your name was Grior?"

"Do nodd be avraid, Hedrunn. I woll do you no halm."

It was like listening to a foreign person trying to speak English when they were just learning it. Hadrian desperately wanted to believe that he would not be 'halmed'

"Who are you, Grior? Where are you from?"

"I gum vrom Joobidir, Hedrun. I am a boy lige you, eggsepd am onli nine eardth yearzz old."

"Jupiter!?" gasped Hadrian, "Really? Jupiter? Wow! Oh.... I'm *eleven* years old."

There was a short silence while the two boys from different parts of the solar system simply looked at each other up and down. Hadrian broke the silence: "What have you put in my head, Grior?"

"Id iz onli an inderplanedary gommunigationn zgrambler, Haidran. Id will nod harm you. Id changes my languaj do yourz when I agdivade and yourz do mine wen you agdivade."

"We call it 'speaking' rather than 'activating' but I think it's the same thing."

"Thiz iz the zame thing. The zgramblerz are nod yedt bervecd budt the more we zpeak, the clearer id will begome, undil id will zoon pe berfecd." This was beyond credulity. On the face of it, Hadrian was standing in his bedroom in the middle of the night, communicating with a boy from Jupiter. He had to be dreaming, surely.

Hadrian stepped a little gingerly towards both his bed and Grior. As he did, Grior rolled slowly to the side so that he was not blocking Hadrian's path. Fear was disappearing fast and curiosity and wonder were starting to dominate Hadrian's thoughts.

Sitting on his bed and trying to maintain eye contact with one eye on a rotating mini-trunk, Hadrian asked the inevitable question-

"Why are you here on planet Earth, Grior?"

No sooner had the words left his lips than he noticed Grior acting oddly. The space boy swung to and fro and his eye darted about all over the place, looking at anything other than Hadrian. It was almost as if Grior was embarrassed. Hadrian felt an odd rasping sound in his head behind the language scrambler. It was the sound of a bee buzzing, mixed with that of a saw being used on wood. Grior's mesh hand was covering his face grille. Seeing Grior's obvious discomfort and hearing that strange sound baffled Hadrian for a minute or so, then it came to him suddenly. Grior was doing the Jupiter equivalent of crying!

"I'm zorry, Hadran, bzzz bzzz. I wizh I bzz bzzzz I waz nodd on earth! Bzzz, bzzz bzzz. I am losd! I levt Jupider by aggzident bzz bzzzz and landed on your moon. Bzzz I had to leave there very gwickly and bzzzzzz landed here." It took Hadrian a moment to absorb all of this information, especially when the fuzzy language was mixed with the buzzing sounds.

"Don't get upset, Grior. I can show you where Jupiter is in an atlas and I'm sure my dad could work out how to get you back there. Are you here all on your own?"

Grior's crying fit seemed to be abating, although not stopping altogether. "Oh, yezz. I'm bzzz alone and cand think bzz how to get back home bzzz. Your vather cannod helb me, Hadrin."

"Perhaps not – but you're not alone now, Grior. I'd

like to be your friend and if I can help in any way, I certainly will."

"I abbreciate your kindnezz, Hadrian, bud before you offer helb you really have to know my ztory. You zee, I did something voolish and lefd Jupidder. As iv thatz nodd enouv, thingz jusd godt worze and worze!"

Suddenly, the upper flap in Grior's torso started making noises which immediately caught Hadrian's attention.

Beeeeeeep pip pip beeeeeeep pip pip beeeeeeep........

"What's that?"

"My enerjy levelz are getting low. I must regenerade."

"How do you do that?"

"On Jupidter I absorb mineralz from our rockz and fluid vrom drenjo."

"Drenjo?"

"You do not have id on earth, Hadran. I don't know whad I'll do without idt".

"What is it like?"

"Id is like a mixdure ov your vegetables, vruit, tree leaves and bushes, I subbose. I've no idea, really. Zat iz as near as I gan thingk."

"We've got fruit and vegetables downstairs and some small rocks and pebbles in the garden we could try!" suggested Hadrian.

"I don't know. Iv I don't take something the bleep will get louder and quicker until it suddenly stops dead.

Then, I just stop altogether until someone else reactivates my system."

"Then it's worth a go, Grior!" said Hadrian, bounding out of bed and stopping at the bedroom door with his hand on the handle. "Wait here, I'll fetch some fruit and vegetables from the kitchen."

Hadrian did a fast creep down the stairs with the stealth of a hunter. He kept to the wall and paused briefly at the bottom to listen for any sounds of parents. He opened the fridge door. Lifting a plastic carrier from the recycling bundle, he popped in two carrots, and, with much delight, six Brussels sprouts from a large bag. That would save him having to suffer them! He closed the fridge and took three potatoes, an onion and an ageing leek from the vegetable rack. Passing the fruit bowl he lifted two apples, a banana and a small orange. That would do for starters. He took the steps two at a time until he reached his bedroom. Grior had rolled over to the window. Hadrian handed him the bulging carrier bag. "I hope you like what....."

But Grior wasn't taking time to consider whether he liked the contents or not as he snatched the bag with his heavy arm.

"Thangk you, thangk you," he said pushing both apples, a potato and a carrot into his upper flap. There was the sound of a food blender with hiccups, punctuated with an occasional grind and squelch. The unpeeled banana, sprouts, second carrot and another potato followed to the same sounds of the stomach orchestra. Grior finalised the moment by pushing in the orange, leek, last potato, onion and then – the carrier bag!

Hadrian opened his mouth to warn him about the carrier, but the blender ground and squelched and hiccupped away until everything was gone, including the bag. The whole process stopped with a hiss like the hydraulic brakes on an articulated lorry.

"Was that all right?"

"It seems to have worked quide a bit, but I will have to transmetabolise myself to one of your earth caves or beaches to try and take in rock minerals. I will need to do thiz soon, Hadrian."

Hadrian noticed that the language was getting clearer and clearer. Grior must have been thinking the same; "Our activation is almost perfect, now Hadrian."

"I was just thinking that. What if I sneaked into the garden and brought you up some pebbles and stones? We've some small rocks too!"

"You are indeed a friend, Hadrian but I would be better to go now. I promise to return tomorrow night to tell you my full story"

"What does transmetabolise mean, Grior?"

"I will vaporise in order to travel without having to crash through walls and obstacles. I will show you, my friend, said Grior. Good night until I return tomorrow night."

As Hadrian reluctantly returned the goodnight wish, Grior started to spin. Slowly at first, he accelerated within three seconds into a barely visible blob of a transparent cling-filmy figure. The curtains puffed up in a much gentler way than when Grior had arrived and the windows shivered slightly. He was gone.

Hadrian sat transfixed for a few moments then crossed to the window. Nothing stirred below. He crossed to the main light switch and flicked it on. He let his gaze wander round the room looking for any sign that Grior had been. There was none. He caught himself in the mirror and looked at his forehead. There was nothing visible, yet he could clearly feel the presence of the interplanetary communication scrambler. Switching off the light, he climbed back into bed, his brain racing with the night's events, his adrenalin in top gear. Reaching up, his thumb pressed the bedside lamp's button and all reverted to pitch blackness.

"Don't know why I'm bothering to lie down... I'll never manage to get any sleep now."

*

CHAPTER 2

The alarm buzzed for ten seconds then automatically switched to the preset radio station. Hadrian's head began to clear to the music of the Rolling Stones belting out 'Paint it Black'. He clapped his hand on the 'stop' button and swung his legs round onto the floor. Radio One should be wakening him with The Arctic Monkeys or some modern band and not one of his dad's old time favourites. What a night! What an incredible dream! He sat on his bed and let his eyes roam, looking for some indication that Grior had really happened in his physical life and not only in his head. There was nothing. His mother had been in and opened his curtains and the new day shone into his room with the sun's early rays making dappled patterns of bright light on his carpet. He gently rubbed fingertips over his forehead but could not feel the presence of any interplanetary scrambler. So it had just been a dream, then. If so, it had been the best dream of his life.

"HAY-DREE-ANN!!" called his mother in a singsong voice.

"CO-MING!" replied our hero in the same way.

The exhilarating aroma of lightly grilled bacon on soft morning rolls wafted upstairs. It had the effect of cutting the duration of Hadrian's visit to the bathroom. He emptied his nagging bladder, dripped a little water onto one half of his right hand and then rubbed both hands together. Having 'washed' his hands he splashed his face and then briefly rushed his toothbrush across his teeth. Ablutions completed, he bounded downstairs towards the kitchen table.

"Sleep well?" asked his mum as usual while wetting his cheek with her customary 'good morning' kiss.

"Yes, thanks," replied Hadrian as his dad ruffled his hair with a hearty "G'morning son! Any MI5 last night?"

"MI5?"

"Yes, bugs in your bed and all that. Ha ha ha ha..." and dad chortled at his crummy joke.

"Never mind MI5, have you been having a midnight feast from the fruit bowl last night?" challenged Mrs Wall.

"That's strange," said Hadrian, "I dreamt I gave fruit to a space boy."

"Space boy indeed! Like father like son. This is your fault Tony, with all your silly jokes. Well, my lad, I hope your space boy doesn't get earthlings' diarrhoea because if he does he'll get no sympathy from me!"

"Yes, indeed," quipped dad, "Fruit is bad for space travellers. You should only give a flying saucer a flying cup. BOOM BOOM!" and dad was away in his own world again.

The fruit was gone, thought Hadrian. Unless Grior had really happened, what could have happened to it? A new excitement stirred deep down. He would have to wait until tonight to find out. Hadrian desperately hoped that Grior *had* actually happened and he left for school that morning wishing the next fifteen hours away.

Morning dragged on interminably. How was he expected to concentrate on spelling and boring activities on mathematical measure when his mind was racing round and round the universe? Eating his packed lunch was more of a contest than a pleasure. He bit off chunks of sandwich distractedly, chewed them over once or twice then swallowed the considerable lumps over a dry throat. Hadrian stared at the empty lunch box and wondered how the apple had become a core, the biscuit an empty wrapper and the drink carton devoid of content. It passed through his mind to feign sickness in order to be sent home, but then considered that time would drag by even more slowly at home. When the afternoon bell shrilled out, he walked in a robotic trance to where he lined up. Only five minutes later, there was a light rap on the classroom door. When Hadrian recognised who it was coming in, he was delighted he had decided to stay.

On Friday afternoons, a parent or grandparent of a

pupil would come into class and tell them about an event, experience or hobby they had. Two weeks ago Kieren's grandad told of some scary moments he'd had while exploring Kenya. That had been brilliant! Last week Mrs Jessiman went on and on about her family's trip to a butterfly farm. Miriam passed round photographs of her mum covered in butterflies of all colours. The first ten minutes were O.K. but after that it was so boring.

This week the twins Craig and Stuart had arranged for their mum to come in and tell about their recent visit to the NASA space station in the USA. At the time of their visit the twins had brought back an autographed poster of Neil Armstrong, the first man to set foot on the moon. Hadrian had showed only polite interest as it was displayed in 'home corner'. Today, he stared with much more intensity into the astronaut's eyes as Mrs Wilkie started to talk. She showed various posters and souvenirs and mixed her presentation with amusing tales from Neil Armstrong and dramatic ones from other members of ground staff in mission control. The afternoon flew by hearing about near disasters, wonderful successes, failures and stories. Mrs Wilkie left five minutes at the end for pupils' questions. Hadrian was bursting to tell someone about Grior but held himself in check while other pupils asked boring questions of her.

At 3.32p.m. Hadrian's feet were pounding the pavement in the direction of home. In his hand he clutched the A4 poster Mrs Wilkie had left in a 'help yourself' heap at the door. The poster was of the 'near' side of the moon and he was sprinting home to have a close study of it. Arriving home like a tornado in the Caribbean, he dashed upstairs to change out of his uniform. While there, he laid the poster on his pillow and then jogged downstairs to his mum, his afternoon snack and to help her prepare for the evening meal.

Having run a couple of errands and set the table, Hadrian popped three doors down to his best pal Robbie's for a game of 'swingball' in the garden. Hadrian was secretly hoping for a glance of Robbie's twelve-year-old sister, Lorna. He absolutely adored her, but would never admit it to anyone, least of all Robbie. She appeared at the door to call Robbie in for tea.

"Hi, Hadrian," she called casually.

If only Hadrian had known that her heart was racing, too, when she called out his name.

"Hi, Lorna. Be seein' ya Robbie!" Hadrian called as he headed home thinking how unattainable Lorna was to the likes of him. 'I wish I was a hero,' he thought as he pushed open his front door.

It was customary for Tony and Jill Wall to tell each other of the kinds of days they'd had while eating dinner. Hadrian would join in sparsely, out of a feeling of obligation. Imagine his parents' pleasant surprise when their son offered the story of his afternoon with enthusiasm.

"Maybe you've uncovered a new interest, darling,"

beamed his mum.

"Not totally new," countered dad, "He's always had his head in the clouds!"

They all laughed, but Hadrian knew that his parents were very pleased with him. As they chatted, he let his mind wander to Lorna. The only time he got a long look at her was when she walked the family spaniel 'Spangles' past his garden. She would stop and chat very briefly while Spangles snuffled restlessly around, if Hadrian happened to be in the garden. He 'happened' to be in the garden any time he saw her leaving her house with Spangles. By the time she reached his gate he would be somewhere in the front garden pretending to be engaged in some task or other. An idea shot into Hadrian's thoughts. What if he had a dog? They could walk both together! God! He would love that! He would swot up on some subjects and talk intelligently to her. He would impress her and they would fall in love. Maybe he would rescue Spangles from some danger and she would kiss him gratefully.

His concentration swung back into the room. Mum was pouring coffee.

"Would you like some dear, now that you're back with us?"

"Sorry, Mum, I…I…was just thinking how great it must be to be an astronaut. Could we get a pet dog, Dad?"

Dad appeared to go deaf when he read the newspaper.

"Tony!..*Tony!*... Antonine Wall, do you hear what your son is asking you!?"

Whenever Jill used his 'Sunday' name, Tony knew it was time to respond.

"A dog, son? A dog? What has brought this on at all?"

"I thought it would be nice and taking it for walks would help keep me fit," started Hadrian.

"But look what happened to our last dog," said Dad.

Hadrian and his mum exchanged glances. They had never had a dog.

"What last dog?" she asked.

"Tut,tut. How can you have forgotten? We went to that international breeder in Auchtermuchty and chose a pedigree Dachshund. Pure German it was."

Mum and Hadrian simply waited for the punch line.

"Our family was complete. There I was, Antonine Wall; you, my dear, who should be known as 'Wailing' Wall, Hadrian Wall and our German dog. We made the mistake of calling him Berlin Wall – and he was knocked down shortly after! BOOM BOOM"

Dad guffawed, mum looked skywards in an expression of exasperation and despite himself, Hadrian chuckled at his father's joke.

"Why don't you just ask Robbie's sister if you can walk their dog with her?" suggested Dad in an effort to finish the conversation." It'd do your street cred a power of good to be seen out with such a pretty thing: and his sister's not bad either! Ha, Ha, Ha!" It worked perfectly.

Hadrian blushed violently without Dad noticing. Mum pretended not to see his discomfort and smiled secretly to herself. Hadrian dried the dishes and watched TV with his parents until he could stand the slow passage of time no more. He popped upstairs and brought down the A4 poster. He spread it out at the kitchen table and studied it.

There wasn't a great deal of detail on it. Several plains known as seas were shown. They had fascinating names such as 'Ocean of Storms', 'Sea of Showers', 'Sea of Moisture', 'Sea of Serenity' and 'Sea of Tranquillity'. Hadrian wondered if Grior had been in any of these areas, if he existed.

"What's so interesting son?" interrupted his dad.

"This poster we got from Stuart and Craig's mum after her talk about NASA. It's the near side of the moon. Who gave the names to all the dry seas on the moon, Dad?"

"I don't know who named them all, son, but I remember Rod Stewart named one the 'Sea Youjimmy'".

Hadrian decided to resume his appreciation of the poster without asking his father anything else. A massive crater called Copernicus was shown as dominating the western area. Hadrian began to wish even more deeply than ever before that he could go there. He looked at some of the other seas, 'Sea of Crises', 'Sea of Fertility' and 'Sea of Nectar'. Why were they called such names? Could something grow in the Sea of Fertility? Would there be drinking water in the Sea of Moisture? The more he analysed the poster the more tangents his mind flew off at and his imagination took over. The Nine o'clock News came on TV. Was it only nine o'clock? Hadrian made his excuses shortly after and said he was going up to play with his PlayStation.

"Don't forget to pack your football kit for your match tomorrow while you're up there."

"Right, Mum."

"I'm doing the transport tomorrow, son. Who else am I taking in the team limo?"

"Oh, I almost forgot, Dad. Robbie, Grant and Johnnie are coming here at ten sharp. We've to report at the ground at quarter past."

"No problem, son."

Hadrian played various games on his PlayStation without paying any attention to any of them. He spent more time squinting at the poster on the floor beside him, just wishing time would pass. He was allowed to stay up later on a Friday and Saturday, but tonight he had showered and changed for bed by ten to ten. He sat up with his moon chart, using the long pointed tool from his Swiss army knife to trace imaginary journeys on the side of the moon visible from earth. What about the other side? Please be real, Grior, Hadrian pleaded mentally in an almost prayer-like fashion. There's so much you could tell me, so much I'd love to know. He set down the chart and knife on his bedside table, deliberately left his lamp on and lay back. He knew he wouldn't sleep, but he would have to be in bed for his mother coming up. He stared at his window, willing Grior to appear. His curtains hung limp. He settled down to wait.

Hadrian's eyes opened. His room was in darkness. His mother must have been in and switched off his lamp. He must have dozed off, although how he managed to do that he didn't know. Swinging his legs over the side, he jumped out of bed and went to the window. He pulled his curtains open wide and stared out. There was nothing happening, really, but there hadn't been anything yesterday either. He waited by the window watching his curtains as much as the view, waiting for them to billow. He waited a long five minutes. He waited a further long three minutes. He began to feel cold and went back to sit on his bed with the duvet pulled up over his shoulders. He switched on his lamp and waited. After ten minutes he stopped himself from falling forward as he almost dozed off. Perhaps the light was preventing Grior coming so he switched it off. He was tired. He clambered back into bed properly, snuggled up into a cosy ball and fell back to sleep.

A slight voice invaded his dreamless sleep.

"Hadrian".

It would be his mum calling him to get up and get ready for his football. The voice got louder until Hadrian suddenly realised he was not hearing it in his ears but in his head.

"Hadrian, Hadrian."

He opened his eyes, clicked on the bedside light and found himself delighting in the wondrous sight that was Grior.

"Hello again, Hadrian," said Grior, covering his face grille.

"Hi, Grior – so you were real after all! Brilliant!"

"Thank you for helping me, my friend," said Grior

"Oh, here, I have something for you," Hadrian reached under his bed and pulled out a bag containing three potatoes, an apple, two carrots and several large pebbles.

"Thank you very much," said Grior feeding them all into his crunching 'feeding' flap, carrier bag and all, once again.

"Did you find some caves to help with your regeneration, last night?"

"I found a wonderful rocky beach where I was able to ingest many minerals. It could sustain me for three earth years, I think."

"That's good news. No doubt you could find it again?"

"Yes, Hadrian, I will use my tracer to show you."

Grior produced a circular screen from his lower flap. It stuck magnetically to the claw on his thick arm while he deftly stroked parts of the frame with the straight 'fingers' of his thin one. He held the screen towards Hadrian. He saw the east coast of northern

England whizzing past as he 'flew' northwards, slowing quickly at Montrose and stopping totally at a shingle beach at a place called Inverbervie.

"Very impressive tracer, Grior! But I suppose it's nothing special to someone who has made it from Jupiter to Earth via the moon."

Grior slipped the tracer back into his flap.

"Talking about Jupiter, what is it like? You promised to tell me your story tonight, Grior."

"Ah, yes, my story. The story of a very stupid and naughty boy, Hadrian. Are you sure you want to hear it?"

"Every detail. Who knows, maybe I'll be able to help you."

Hadrian settled back into a comfortable seated position and gave Grior his full attention.

"First I tell you a little about my planet. You might think that we are mostly gas and liquid, with only a small rocky core. If you were able to get under the hydrogen and helium curtain swirling round our planet you would find that we have used heat and magnetism to produce metallic hydrogen. We have a sophisticated system of fused rocks from our hard core and from our space farming. These two sources form the basis of construction materials for our buildings and our regeneration needs. You would call regeneration resources 'food', on Earth. We have farmed extensively on Miranda, one of Uranus's moons. If you ever see it you will see that we have removed much of it and shipped its rock chunks to our home planet.

Once scientists in your planet – or others – discover how we harness hydrogen, liquids and our magnetic forces to manufacture sophisticated materials, then the secret of our existence will be secret no longer. For the moment, Earth scientists do not believe our planet can sustain any intelligent form of existence and we are very happy to remain secret. Now you know a little of the mysteries of Jupiter, I will tell you my sad tale."

*

CHAPTER 3

Grior rolled to the window, swivelled his 'eye' round to look at Hadrian and began.

"I was made by Eneku. On earth he would be my dad, although we don't have mothers. Eneku, my dad, is a brilliant space scientist. For seven earth years he and his team have been working on a revolutionary method of space travel for individual planetiks."

"Planetiks?"

"People, Hadrian. Your equivalent would be people. Two of your years ago they made their first breakthrough with the Kapsule, a pod which transports an individual through space. It is ingenious. You would bite into the pod – we feed it into our flap – and a thick, sticky liquid flows into you and immediately sprouts a protective coating all over you. This coating can withstand tremendous heat and severe cold and propels its passenger at incredible speeds. From here you would travel to your moon in less than one earth hour."

"One hour?!" gasped Hadrian, "It takes longer than

that to get to my Uncle Geoff's in York!"

"Yes. The Transporter Kapsule is a truly wonderful invention. One year ago Eneku went on planetary transvision to explain to all dwellers about the invention. His team had tested the space travel pods on domestic pet robots such as agremoes and trugers. I can't explain what they are, you don't have anything like them on earth. They were launched and have been tracked to Uranus and Neptune. They had time switches programmed into their horns, in the case of the agremoes, and into the tails of the trugers and were programmed to return a few earth days later. They returned safely. Happy screeching could be heard all over Jupiter and the transvisor in our home was buzzing with compliments and questions and excitement."

Hadrian was bubbling to ask questions about the robot pets and transvision but was spellbound listening to Grior's tale.

"I had never seen anything like it, Hadrian. I was so proud of my father. He even got a transcom from Quorum One, the leader of our planet! Imagine how I felt, then, Hadrian, when my dad recently told me he had been invited to personally address all Quorum members, top space scientists and Macrothinkers about a top secret development he and his team had just perfected. He was to go to the Arena Centre where he would take Quorum One and the other Importances on a tour of the laboratories, while almost 1000 dwellers would sit in the arena and watch the tour on Screensee.I was so delighted for him at the time, but now I wish it had never happened."

"What could be greater than the travel capsule, Grior?"

"The Universe Bag, Hadrian, the Universe Bag."

Grior swivelled and rolled nearer to the bed, bending his eye trunk so that he still looked at Hadrian.

Hadrian experienced a strange sensation through his forehead, as if registering Grior's sadness.

"I begged my father to take me with him. I had often been to his labs, so knew all about safety and behaviour issues. I had helped him with simple tasks such as extracting ores from common rock and laser-slicing segments of planet core. After a detailed warning of how particularly important perfect behaviour and safety awareness would be, he agreed to let me accompany him!"

Grior did a slow mini-circuit in the middle of the room and stopped immediately in front of Hadrian, the closest they had been so far.

"It was magnificent, Hadrian. The Arena was packed with excited beings. The Institute for Research was lit up with multi-coloured laser light darts, flashes of luminous crystal palettes and bursts of atmosfire. The convoy of control discs entered the arena. My dad and I rolled on the first one with the great thinker Makromensar, space scientists Dij and Volra – and our magnificent planet controller, Quorum One himself. Once all the dignitaries were on their discs, the guide disc glided into position in front of us and locked us on to its tracker."

Hadrian wasn't even sure if he was understanding everything Grior was telling him, but he had a vivid picture in his mind of how he thought things were in the story.

Grior continued, "The procession floated once round the arena to tumultuous metal banging and high-pitch noised emissions – like your applause. The guide disc led us into the institute and straight for my father's lab. My head was swivelling in great excitement. The laser screen dissolved and we entered the lab. There, on a work slab surrounded by security plasma lay the most beautiful collection of crystal bars I had ever seen."

"I *wish* it had been me, Grior."

Grior's eye swept in an arc and continued to sway to and fro as he continued:

"I wish it *hadn't* been me, my friend! There were 10 bars glittering with astonishing beauty in the bag; a Mars crimson one, an Earth lime green, a Mercury blue, a Neptune yellow one, a Venus amber, a Jupiter purple, a dark green for Uranus, Saturn's turquoise, Pluto pink and a clear one for the moons."

At this, Grior plunged his pincered arm into his top body flap and produced a partly used clear crystal and a chipped lime green one. These immediately dazzled Hadrian and made his mouth say "Wowee!" without him realising it.

Hadrian just gazed at them and impatiently waited

for Grior to tell more.

"The control discs spun round in a slow circle while everyone marvelled at the site and the scene was trans-sent to Screensee outside.

My dad slipped down from our disc when it came to rest and beckoned me to follow. We slipped through the plasma using our entry sounds and found ourselves in beside the full display of crystals and travel pods. And there I stood proudly, while I watched my father explain the research experiment to the greatest and wisest on Jupiter. He amused them with stories of things that had gone wrong at various stages. He captured them with the brilliance of the work of his team had done to produce a different crystal for each planet in the solar system and one for the moons. He explained to a rapt audience that one snap of a bar into our regeneration system would enable us to travel to the planet the crystal represented, in a space travel pod. Secret rehearsals had seen robots sent to Saturn and back and to our moon Io. The most recent adventure had seen a space robot successfully sent to Uranus, then Io and home again. There were gasps of appreciation from everyone, including Quorum One when they heard that."

"These crystals? Can take you to planets? This is incredible, Grior!"

Hadrian stroked the beautiful part-used crystals which Grior had laid on his bed.

"Wouldn't be much use to me, though, there's no way my teeth could bite crystal and I definitely couldn't chew it," Hadrian sighed. He had been starting to think of all kinds of wonderful opportunities such crystals could offer him. He could go to Jupiter with Grior and see it for himself. He would have to tell his parents, of course and that might be tricky. Perhaps they could all go? He was snapped from his reverie by Grior.

"You can bite them Hadrian, I'll explain in a moment, when I finish my story. My dad ended with; 'And so, my esteemed importances, colleagues and audience, if my son Grior will just hold up the bag.....Open it..... Pour in the travel pods......close the bag. You are now looking at the complete kit for exploring the solar system.'

The applause continued for a long time, then the screencast was faded down so that only the dignitaries were left. A laser shield faded to reveal a buffet of various sizes of drenjo, rocks of varying crumblability, slices of planet core and other delicacies for the importances to enjoy. The plasma vapourised and we were out among the others. Normally I would have been straight for the buffet, but I was still holding the bag and was trying to take in what I had just heard. That was when I overheard the remark which made me do something stupid.

Two Quorum members were discussing the crystals. Member K said, 'It all sounds wonderful H, but it's all very well sending robots. Would Eneku send a higher-order being? What about his son Grior? Would he wrap him in a pliable cover and send *him* to Io?'

'Indeed, K; but never mind Io, would he risk propelling him to our largest moon?'

'What, Ganymede, H? I hardly think so. The boy would get lost in our huge moon!'

I was furious! How dare they speak like that about a scientist twice as intelligent as both of them added together! I opened the bag and retrieved the clear crystal and a travel capsule. Making certain that K and H were watching, I swallowed the pod and snapped a chunk of the crystal into my feedflap. As I did this I heard them both shout out and my dad spin round to face me. A thought flashed. What if it was a different moon and not Io. Planet Earth had a moon. What if the crystal took me there? As I lost awareness I heard my father shout that the last moon I thought of was the one I would visit. I had been thinking of your moon and that's where I landed."

"That's a brilliant, fantastic story Grior. For all you say, I still wish it was me! But how does that help me bite the crystal?"

"I was just about to finish by telling you that. A Makrothinker asked that very question to my dad. Dwellers on my planet are of different grades and have different capabilities. How would trugers, for instance, manage? They have soft leathery feed hatches and can ingest only the softest grade drenjo and the jelly-like substance called sleed.

My father explained that when you present the crystal for ingestion you imagine what you would like it to be. As you break it, it will become whatever you choose, in taste and texture."

"So if I imagined this moon crystal to be a biscuit, it would be a biscuit when I bit it?"

"Yes, Hadrian."

"A ginger snap? Chocolate digestive?"

"Whichever you want, Hadrian."

Hadrian let out a long whistle of appreciation and stared at the green and clear sparkling space tickets on his duvet. He stroked the clear one and thought 'You are a moonbiscuit'.

"Do you have the rest of the Universe Bag in your flap?"

"I wish I did. Do you remember last night I told you I had to leave your moon in a hurry? Well, I met two different life forms on the moon: The friendly Dugiri and the very unfriendly Zapro. The Dugiri are very like little earth fruit balls. They have a tough, knobbly skin with some green fronds and are a dusty, mainly orange/red colour."

"Sounds like something I once saw in TESCOs. It was called dragon fruit!" interjected Hadrian. Grior seemed to be scanning his system for an idea of TESCO and dragon fruit.

"Yes, that is a very good comparison for size, appearance and texture, Hadrian. They skim along the surface and can move at good speeds. I could not keep up with them with my rollsphere bumping on the rocky surface. Their main purpose is to grow and then explode themselves, revealing a clump of wet stringy haspira, a substance which you ingest and it enables you to breathe if you need to and provides a replacement for food and liquids too. Their leader was Jurgat and he was larger than the others."

"So there are creatures on the moon after all. What about the nasty ones?"

"I didn't have time to find out about them, really. I was resting, showing Jurgat and the Dugiri the crystals. I was trying to explain about the Universe Bag and was holding up a handful of travel pods, the clear crystal which had brought me to their moon and the lime green one. I told them the green one would take them to Earth. Everyone was so attentive we were caught unawares. There was a sudden shout of 'Zapro!!' and these large V-shaped creatures came zooming in to attack. One of them was W-shaped. He was the leader and was coming at me. Jurgat screamed out, 'It is Lantar the evil one. Roll away or you will be destroyed!!'

Dugiri were zigzagging and Zapro were in amongst them. I felt the Universe Bag slip out of my hand and hit the dust. Lantar was almost within reach of me. I could see he had three vicious heads.

As he reached me he intercepted a Dugiri in mid-flight and scrunched him in the jagged metal teeth of his middle head. I did not want to be destroyed. Lantar snatched up the bag with his left head and I decided my only hope was to flap a pod and crunch some green crystal. I did, just as the stinking fumes from his heads closed in on me. I blanked out and when I materialised, I was in your room.

And that is the story of how I came here. Luckily I have three pods here and the two crystals. I shall have to go back to get the bag, or I can't get home."

Grior's eye trunk drooped sadly and Hadrian didn't even notice. He was too excited taking in the information about living things on the moon. After nearly two minutes, Hadrian sat bolt upright and asked, "Grior, please let me go back for you. It would be the adventure of a lifetime for me! I'll take my Swiss Army knife and Powersling – a catapult which fires ball bearings at a fierce pressure. The atmosphere is much thinner than here and I could bound along quicker than you could roll. I beg you Grior, please let me go!"

Grior was not at all sure, but was certainly not keen to go back himself.

"It is too dangerous, my friend. This is my problem. No-one fights on Jupiter. I don't know what to do and I would be easily destroyed. My hope is that my father will send a search party."

"But that could take ages! He doesn't know which moon you targeted and certainly has no idea that you have come here."

As if to influence Grior, Hadrian opened his bedside drawer and laid out his sturdy catapult and a rattling bag of metal balls. His hand dipped into the drawer again and retrieved his knife. He started pulling out the various blades and attachments to impress Grior and set the fully fanned-out knife down beside the Powersling. He carefully laid his poster of the moon down beside his weapons and looked searchingly at his space friend.

"Please let me help you get back home to Jupiter. We fight all the time on Earth and I'm good at it!"

Grior rolled round in little circles. He seemed agitated. His eye was examining every detail of Hadrian as if weighing up the pros and cons of his dilemma.

"Are you certain you want to do this?"

"Yes, Grior. Absolutely certain."

Hadrian went to his wardrobe without another word and put on a black T-shirt, jeans, hoodie and trainers. He took a sheet of paper from his printer and wrote a note to his parents: 'Dear Mum and Dad, Felt like a long early morning jog. Didn't want to wake you. Will be back later. Love, Hadrian xx'. He stuck the note on his monitor screen with Blu Tac.

"A bit of insurance, Grior." He then jotted down the colours of the crystals for each planet on the back of his poster.

Hadrian filled his hoodie pockets with the ball bearings, the knife and map and made himself as tall as he could standing 'toe to toe' with Grior. Two boys from opposite ends of the solar system just stood in silence, staring at each other. He slipped the catapult into the back pocket of his jeans.

Still they stood. Hadrian lifted two travel pods and pocketed one of them for the return journey. As Grior watched uncomfortably, he slipped the sparkling green into a deep pocket. "Hadrian, I am not sure about this."

"Grior, I can fight. I have weapons and a map. I can take advantage of the thin atmosphere to travel much faster than you. I am taller. I am desperate to go on this adventure to make friends with flying fruit and fight Vs and Ws, two letters from our alphabet. I want to help you, my friend."

"You are very brave, Hadrian. I will worry about you, so be quick." Grior rolled up to Hadrian and rested his thin arm on Hadrian's shoulder. Grior's sharp hand actually nipped Hadrian. It seemed like an accident but was no such thing.

"I'm off before you change your mind. What will you do if by any chance I don't get back?"

"There are plenty rocks on Inverbervie beach. I will pack myself with these and wait to pick up transmitted signals from any search party. There is a huge food stock. I will be fine."

"See you at breakfast then!" Hadrian bit into the pod and swallowed a tasteless suspension the colour of guava juice. He bit into the clear crystal and found himself eating a delicious moonbiscuit tasting of chocolate-covered ginger. His mind shut down into temporary suspension and he was away.

*

CHAPTER 4

Hadrian's space travel pod propelled itself through earth's atmosphere and into space in the twinkling of an eye. He was aware that he wasn't conscious, but somehow he was registering what was happening. Or was he registering an optical illusion?

Was what he saw real or was it like a space dream to pass away the flight? He saw vivid images of various moons from all over the solar system as he sped towards his destination. He had no way of telling if his eyes were open or closed, whether he was actually observing this incredible scene or just registering a space dream in his mind. He could feel vibrations in his forehead from the interplanetary communication scrambler. He could not move a muscle. Two tiny moons zapped by and he found himself having their names projected into his brain. 'Phobos' and 'Demos'. If he had been at school and teacher asked him to name some moons, he would only have been able to identify Earth's moon. He could now include Io, thanks to Grior, but he had never before heard of Phobos or Demos. He felt a tug as the pod adjusted its flight path.

Swimming into his vision next came a huge moon which Hadrian was about to identify as the Earth's when his head told him 'Ganymede'. He was looking at the biggest moon in the solar system as it floated close to his eyes in his dream state. It was another of Jupiter's moons and looked very like Hadrian supposed the Earth moon would if close up. Just as he was starting to think about Ganymede, it faded in favour of the volcanic Io.

It rushed through his consciousness until Titan, Saturn's largest moon, floated by wearing its orange clouds. Hadrian wondered if his pod was like a space bus, working through the moons like bus stops until it reached his destination. This feeling only increased when a succession of Uranus's moons rattled by in quick succession, Oberon, Titania, Umbriel, Ariel and the odd-shaped Miranda, which looked as if it had been subjected to a space war. It was roughly egg-shaped with massive chunks missing from its surface. This was the moon Grior had mentioned the Jupitarians – if that was what they were called – were farming. As soon as the Earth's moon ventured into his mind picture, even just as a small button in the distance, he recognised it for certain. As it approached, the whole space 'dream' became three dimensional, his pod seemed to lose speed until he slipped out of the mind show and into witnessing the orbiting of the moon. Hadrian was of no doubt that his eyes were opened now, as he watched the moon surface slip by below. This was totally fascinating.

Suddenly, he was above the far side of the moon and expected to have to adjust his eyes to the plunge into the blackness of what people called the dark side of the moon. To his astonishment he saw sunlight playing extensively across the surface of this far side. The Earth may never see this side but it was not dark because it still benefited from the sun's light.

No sooner was he considering this than he started to emerge back onto the near side. He was much nearer to the moon's surface and could see a beautiful 'earthrise' happening while skimming over craters, cinder cones, small mountains and other surface features. Hadrian felt dizzy. He still couldn't move. He was aware of further slowing down. He tried to open his eyes and concentrate. He could feel his concentration slipping. He passed out. While Hadrian was unconscious, the travel pod hit the surface at 320 mph at an inclined, nose-up angle of $27°$ to the horizontal and then it bounced and embarked on a huge sweeping anti-clockwise arc over the area just to the west of the Sea of Serenity. As it whizzed past the Sea of Tranquillity at 210mph it maintained a height of 10feet above the surface. As it slowed to 130mph, its arc turned it further away from the northern tip of the Sea of Nectar towards the Sea of Moisture. The travel pod landed with a high-speed skid, bearing an unconscious Hadrian Wall into the no-man's area of land between these two 'seas'. A cloud of soft dust puffed up and drifted away in wispy suspension.

The pod cooled immediately and ejected Hadrian's inert form onto the nearby surface with a gentle nudge. Its job done, the pod immediately started to implode until it had vaporised without trace.

Hadrian's subconscious system sprang into action and immediately spiralled him upwards into consciousness. An oxygen bubble had automatically triggered on landing and was stuck over his mouth and nose. The bubble was graduated and showed three hours supply. Hadrian sat up slowly and stared. A shiver of fear and excitement coursed through his body. He stood up and marvelled at the sight of the Earth out there in space. His parents were there, and Robbie, and Lorna! If only she could see him! And Grior, of course. Thinking of his friend brought him back to his senses. The Universe Bag! How on earth would he start to look for it? He smiled as he thought of how his father would have quipped, "On Earth you won't start to look for it, Hadrian. On the *moon* you will."

Hadrian felt a lump in his throat when he thought about his mum and dad out there on earth while he was alone on the moon. What if this adventure went all wrong and he didn't ever get home?

Would his bed just be empty? Would they think he had been abducted and start a manhunt for his kidnapper? His parents would have to go on TV and appeal for his safe return and all the time he'd be lost in space. Offering to help Grior seemed a bit hasty now that he thought of it. After all he could just have introduced him to his parents and kept him as a pet until he was eventually rescued. That seemed a much more sensible solution, sitting alone on the moon, gazing across to the Earth. He sighed deeply. "Well it's what you wanted." He spoke out loud to himself, if only to have his voice for company. He stood up easily and started making huge, effortless jumps round and round. He laughed loud and started doing aerial somersaults and back flips. After a few minutes he pulled himself up into serious thought. 'This won't get Grior's bag and is just using up my oxygen. I'd better do *something* to start the search before my air runs out. I wonder if I'll meet any Dugiri with a supply of haspira?'

He fished out his poster of the moon and tried to make sense of it. He was smoothing it out when a sharp sting shot through his thumb. It wasn't very painful really but had surprised him. It seemed to come from the poster. He cautiously ran his middle finger over the poster. When it passed over the crater Copernicus, he felt it again. He tested it again with his forefinger and sure enough he got the jab at the same crater and nowhere else.

"Right, that's it. I'm heading for Copernicus," stated Hadrian loudly, "but how can I be sure I'm holding the poster pointing in the correct direction?"

He turned round to face another direction and he repeated the experiment. This time there was no stab.

He tried another position with the same outcome. Turning back to his original position, he ran his little finger lightly over the page and, a little timidly, touched Copernicus. The stab was strong again.

"That's it, then. I head for Copernicus, in this direction." Hadrian pocketed the map, checked pockets to confirm crystals, capsule, knife, catapult and ammunition and then started off with long leisurely bounds in what he hoped was the right direction. He should be all right if he kept the Earth behind him and checked his poster map regularly. He pretended to be running in the moon Olympics and leapt along playing the Proclaimers' 'Five Hundred Miles' in his head.

Just as he was about to set a new solar system record for lunar leaping he got the fright of his life when about twenty flying dragon fruit whizzed past him, circled him as he slowed down and were instantaneously joined by several others, many just hovering at various heights and distances, apparently taking him in. Hadrian slowed and then stopped running altogether. He stood still and examined these odd things buzzing about him. "You must be Dugiri. Grior told me about you."

The dragon fruits were whizzing round him, over him, between his open legs, behind him, in front of him and above him. They made a wind-whistle sort of sound as they zipped about. It reminded Hadrian of the sound he could make by blowing gently across the neck of an empty milk bottle. No matter how fast the Dugiri moved they never clashed into each other. Another thing Hadrian noticed was that they could stop dead from any speed. If Grior hadn't told him some things about them Hadrian might well have been frightened by the frenzy of movement and how close they came to him. He had no doubt that if one of them came at him at full speed – whatever that was – the impact could kill him. They were like a swarm of red ball bees round him and seemed to be increasing in number although it was impossible to count them. Hadrian thought he'd try communicating again.

"Grior told me you were very friendly and helpful: Especially your leader, Jurgat." He felt a tingly vibration in his forehead and heard the sounds.

"Gsh frow shee mm zp."

Oh, no, he thought, the scrambler isn't working!

As he was wondering how to cope with this setback, a gap appeared in the swarm in front of him and a fruit twice the size of the others drifted slowly towards his face. It was deeper red than the others and had more knobbly bits all over it. Some of the knobbles had green strands flowing from them, though it looked as if some had been knocked off. Some of the smaller creatures had full sets of green fronds on the hard raised bits of their flesh. Some had none and others had some. Perhaps they grow them as they mature or lose them in battle, thought Hadrian.

"Jurgat!" said Hadrian, smiling at the large Dugiri. Its diameter was roughly the length of a school ruler, about 30cms, while the others were half that width.

"Gsh frow shee mm zp," repeated the ball as it drifted up from Hadrian's waist height to his chin, eyes and then forehead. Hadrian stood stock still and had a careful look as the creature moved slowly up past his face. There was no sign of any face, or parts of one. Hadrian felt the ball exert gentle, steady pressure on his head. After some seconds like this, he heard

"Grior. How shee mm zp."

He felt the pressure increase slightly and then, "Grior how you know him." Satisfied that the two languages were properly unscrambled, the ball withdrew to a point about a metre in front of Hadrian and remained suspended at his face level.

"Grior escaped from your battle with the Zapro and reached Earth." Unnecessarily, Hadrian pointed to the Earth as he spoke. "My name is Hadrian and I live on Earth. Grior landed in my house. I've come to try and get his bag of crystals back for him."

"Grior escape so pleases us. I Jurgat yes Hadrian. Dugiri yes we will after you take care."

Hadrian smiled and thanked them all. They were all bobbing to and fro like rocking horses, with a few of them completing somersaults. Those with fronds were bowing them like a one-stringed violin and producing high pitched squeaky sounds. Hadrian presumed these were all friendly expressions and so raised both arms and waved to all the Dugiri because, quite frankly, he didn't know quite what to do.

Jurgat spoke, "Hadrian to Copernicus our home. Plan Zapro attack Grior's bag back."

"That's wonderful! Thanks Jurgat. Thanks all of you!"

Without further ado, Jurgat swivelled and headed off at a steady speed with the Dugiri playfully somersaulting and dipping as they sped after him. Hadrian headed off and although he could make substantial leaps with minimal effort, it was all he could to keep apace. The Dugiri were obviously moving at less than half their maximum speed. Some hung back and travelled alongside his shoulders, rolling slightly from side to side and occasionally doing back flips. Hadrian realised the slight side to side movements were in imitation of his shoulder movements as he bounded along. The little rascals were poking fun at him and he laughed with them.

The journey was long and Hadrian was beginning to pant, even though he could zoom almost effortlessly through the low gravity of the moon. He was able to observe his hosts a little as he flowed along among them. They seemed to be communicating by running two of their fronds across each other like a violinist playing a one-stringed violin. They varied the pitch of the resultant squeaking sound by moving the fronds differently and producing a communication system which was not registering on his scrambler. He wondered how those with one or no fronds managed. A quick glance at his oxymeter showed that he was using his air up much more quickly than if he was relaxed and that it showed only 46mins left. He hoped this wet, stringy substance called haspira was all that Grior said it was. He also hoped the Dugiri had some for him!

On they sped, relentlessly heading for Copernicus. A dust storm whirled up in front of the group and caused instant excitement. The Dugiri swarmed towards it and once in amongst the swirling wind they started ingesting the dust through their skins, like miniature vacuum cleaners sucking the storm away from the atmosphere. Jurgat glided over and joined Hadrian.

"Dugiri jellop make from dust. In with dust out comes the jellop. Jellop young Dugiri need to grow. Hadrian see soon". At this he spurted away to the head of the flying flock and its adopted leaping earthling. Hadrian was getting very low on oxygen and wondered if he should mention it.

As if reading his mind, Jurgat brought the swarm to a halt a few minutes later. They formed a rough semi-circle in front of Hadrian. Some rested, some hovered and some shifted position in short darts from A to B and sometimes back again. Jurgat spoke out.

"Soon be home. Hope Dugiri not slowing Hadrian!" At this, the flying fruit balls somersaulted, backflipped, rotated rapidly in clockwise and anti-clockwise spins and made a medley of sounds with their fronds. Hadrian realised he was being teased again. He knew the Dugiri would have been home by now if they hadn't been waiting for him. He joined in the fun by leaping up as best he could to somersault and backflip, much to the Dugiri's enjoyment. He spread his arms and legs ballerina-style, bringing an increased frenzy of enjoyment to his hosts. Soon, however, he started to wheeze as his oxygen started to fail.

"Need haspira, please," he pleaded as he ripped the Oxybubble from his face and cast it aside. It floated gently away and was subjected to many inquisitive nods and prods as it went. At a signal from Jurgat, eight or nine frondless creatures hovered. At the slightest dip from their leader, two of them hurtled towards a large protruding rock and smashed into it at full speed. Their skins exploded and split into countless pieces, leaving two piles of wet, stringy bundles of what could only be described as balls of soggy strips of green noodles at Hadrian's feet.

"Haspira. Ingest now."

Hadrian bent down and grabbed a dripping handful. There was no question of not taking it. He had to breathe. As he raised it to his mouth he found himself almost praying that it wouldn't taste of Brussels sprouts. He was pleasantly surprised to taste something like chicken noodle soup and swallowed the first bunch without much chewing. He scooped up the rest and chewed it a little more this time before swallowing it over. It was only then that it dawned on him that he had just witnessed two Dugiri end their existences for him.

"Is that the only way to get Haspira, Jurgat? It seems horribly cruel for two of you to have to die painfully every time I need it!"

"Not understand 'die'. We make haspira. Dugiri with fewer fronds, better haspira. No fronds at all, perfect haspira.

We have pain never. Pain is Earth thing, not Dugiri."

Hadrian's breathing was deep and slow and was not laboured at all. He had a complete feeling of wellbeing, as if he had just satisfied his thirst, had a large meal and a perfect shower. He felt good. He made a mental note to try and take a sample of haspira home. What seemed like ten easy minutes later Hadrian was aware of an excited buzz in the swarm. He peered ahead to see part of the imposing rocky perimeter of the crater Copernicus. He had arrived at the home of the Dugiri. He soon scaled the steep side of the crater and stared in disbelief at the scene which he saw below.

CHAPTER 5

The crater was enormous, stretching much further than the eye could see. As Hadrian stepped slowly down the terraced steps which nature had fashioned round the surrounding rock wall, his eyes feasted on the scene below. It was organised chaos. The returning Dugiri were buzzing like bees all over an extensive area below. It was laid out in neat plots of yellowish mud. Growing in this mud were hundreds, maybe a thousand tiny Dugiri. They were like yellowish-orange table-tennis balls. They seemed rooted to their spots, but each vibrated rapidly until an adult Dugiri paused over it in flight and oozed jellop out through its skin all over and round the 'baby'. When enough jellop had been deposited the table-tennis ball stopped vibrating and settled contentedly to feed off the goo.

As Hadrian walked between the rows of huge plots, Jurgat floated alongside explaining what was happening. As they reached a secluded area behind an outcrop of crater wall, the same scene unfolded. This time the growing Dugiri were snooker-ball size and the mud they nestled in was deep orange in colour. These were obviously more mature and they displayed signs that they were developing the knobbly parts of their skin.

A cluster of seven jagged rocks ranging from about ten to fifteen metres high protruded from the crater floor. Groups of Dugiri were performing what looked like formation dive-bombing, with wave after wave shattering at full speed against the rocks. An ever-increasing stock of haspira was being produced.

"Why are you making so much haspira, Jurgat?" asked Hadrian, thinking that there was already enough there to feed an army. He still could not believe that the Dugiri felt no pain, especially as he had witnessed that they had emotions when they were teasing him and having fun as his expense.

"Darkbeast come soon. Needs much. Must get ready."

"Darkbeast?"

"Good friend creature. Hadrian see soon. Come with Jurgat see caves." Jurgat floated ahead and disappeared into a fissure in the crater wall. Hadrian followed and once inside the passage widened considerably, opening into a massive cave. The floor was strewn with tennis ball-size Dugiri, growing in a deep red glop. There were numerous cracks and passages in the walls, housing clusters, pairs and single red, knobble-skinned creatures which were obviously near to being fully grown. As he walked carefully along,

Hadrian noticed one or two red, fully fronded 'balls' shake free from the glop and immediately blend with the other flying specimens. At the deepest part of the cave a steady stream of Dugiri hovered at the narrow mouth of a side chamber. Jurgat flew in but Hadrian could only peer in through the small 'window'. It took his eyes a few minutes to discern anything at all. All at once he saw a huge Dugiri, slightly bigger than Jurgat, being constantly drenched in jellop as it moved slowly round the chamber. Jurgat came back out, saying, "Pintar. Leader when Jurgat make self haspira."

Hadrian marvelled at these creatures. They appeared to be simple flying fruits but they had a system of hunting to provide for their young. They all seemed to co-operate with rearing and tending the developing Dugiri and gave up their existence to make haspira without hesitation. He surveyed the busy scene of dashing, vibrating, hurtling, soaking and exploding going on all around. He wished until his heart ached that his dad could be here to see this with him.

As Hadrian watched in wonder a large, dark bulky shape entered the crater from over the edge some 60 metres from him. 'Darkbeast! It has to be!' he thought. He stood still and watched as this stocky creature waddled gorilla-style over the floor of the crater. It generated a reasonable speed and at that distance it reminded Hadrian of the gorillas in the film, 'The Planet of the Apes'. Hadrian was certain the beast had seen him and sure enough, it changed direction and started to edge towards him until it was only about ten metres away.

Its skin seemed to be a strange mixture of plastics, metal and what looked like leather. It was almost as if someone had stitched a patchwork skin for it. It stood nearly twice the height of Hadrian and was much bulkier. It seemed to have two thick legs, a torso, gorilla-type arms and a head. It was covered in plastic and leathery sections and all that Hadrian could see were two deep brown eyes staring at him. The 'face' had no nose, mouth or ears but was just a globe of odd rigid materials and two unblinking eyes.

For what seemed like an eternity he stood as Darkbeast gave him the once over. Snuffling noises were coming from inside the beast as it examined every bit of Hadrian's being.

"Hi, I'm Hadrian – from Earth." No response was forthcoming and so they stood in watchful silence again. Suddenly, examination over, Darkbeast lumbered with a clumsy gait over to the pile of haspira and started to ingest huge quantities of it into a wide kangaroo pouch on its lower torso.

What an appetite it seemed to have! It was only when the beast swung the pouch round onto its back that Hadrian realised that it hadn't been ingesting it at all but was packing it into a sort of back pack made of identical material to its body. Darkbeast gave a quick glance over its left shoulder at Hadrian and then shuffled over to the table tennis balls and scooped an armful up.

It scurried over to the outcrop and started to 'plant' the small balls into the feeding gel of the snooker balls. It repeated this a few times, with Jurgat hovering close to its right shoulder throughout. It then scooped up some 'snooker balls' and disappeared into the fissure in order to plant them in the cave. When Darkbeast emerged from the cavern wall for a fourth time, it did not head back for more. This time it ambled over to the spot where the Dugiri had been smashing themselves into haspira. It painstakingly sought out remnants of skin from the shattered creatures.

It lifted several little pieces, made its way to the goo plots and proceeded to plant these little knobbly chips into the yellowish growing gel.

Hadrian realised he was witnessing the entire cycle of the existence of the Dugiri: little chips growing into table tennis size creatures, then entering phase two to snooker ball size and then into the cave for the final stages, development of fronds and flight. Hadrian ambled round in awe until Darkbeast emerged suddenly from behind a cluster of rocks, threw one glance at Hadrian without breaking stride and headed off into the distance towards the far side of the moon. Jurgat came alongside.

"Dugiri help now find Grior bag."

He dropped to hover near the ground and used two of his fronds to dust draw the moon in front of Hadrian's feet. He marked Copernicus and shaded part to indicate the far side. He marked a cross. "Zapro here.

Bad creatures. Fight, steal Dugiri and destroy us. Why, Hadrian?"

"I don't know Jurgat, I'm sorry."

***

Lantar surveyed his troops with pride. It was time to raid the Dugiri again. His masters on Pluto would be pleased at the progress he had made in preparing for the colonisation of Earth's moon.

Being a Space Commander was an honour. Lantar recalled the day he was set his task by Plutar the All-Powerful, Commander of Planet, its Moons and Colonies, four short years ago.

"Lantar, our planet has been deflected into a rogue orbit around the Golden Star. Pluto will become unbearably cold for 5 ages [1000 earth years]. Our migratory frosts will become solid ice, our basins and craters too cold to regenerate us and the balance of gases in our atmosphere will change to an unfavourable mix. We must evacuate our planet until it rejoins its original orbit.

Space Commanders must take colonisation armies and prepare sites for us. In 4 − 5 smalltimes [4 − 5 earth years] we will send planet ships of settlers to the newly-prepared colonies. You must be ready for us."

"Ready and waiting impatiently, Omniscience!" replied Lantar.

"You have the most important mission, Lantar. You

must set up on the moon of the planet Earth. Establish yourelf on the far side away from Earth so you can develop in secret. This will be a temporary colony. From its moon we will conquer the Earth and make it our main refuelling, repair and development base. Go select your space force and make preparations to go. Take the touch of Plutar with you." At this, Plutar 'bit' Lantar on his neck, leaving the mark of the leader permanently there.

Standing on the Earth's moon, Lantar used two of his heads to look at the branded tattoo he now proudly sported on his central neck. His heads swivelled round independently, surveying his 'V' shaped soldiers. He was aware that he would have to watch SS93 (space soldier 93) who was starting to develop the third neck between the other two. Only the leader was a 'W' and Lantar was that leader. He would pick the moment to disable 93 and destroy him. He could have no threat to his leadership. When he struck, it would be swift and sure. Lantar would also ensure none of 93s allies were nearby to help him. The three eyes on his left neck noticed the huge hillock of haspira they had been stockpiling ready for Plutniks from the planet ships to arrive. Another head focussed on the Pulser inside the spacecraft which had brought Lantar here 4 years ago. The Pulser was sending out a beacon signal towards Pluto in the hope that a planet ship would pick up the signal, lock in and be drawn to the moon.

Hadrian had not yet seen Lantar. He would have

this dubious pleasure much sooner than he thought. His first sight of Lantar would be when he unexpectedly enters Copernicus with a band of his warriors. He would see a 'W'-shaped creature approximately 6 feet tall, with a domed-shaped head at the top of each neck. One central eye glaring from the middle of the head, with two smaller ones providing wide peripheral vision. The eyes are the amber colour of traffic lights. He would notice that other Zapros have but two necks. They are flexible and work independently from each other. Zapro heads can hinge at any point round the rims of their necks. They open to reveal an evil war machine of a mouth, with razor-sharp, vampire-shaped teeth on top and a slicer instead of teeth at the bottom. The slicer can cut through bone as if it was jelly. If a Dugiri gets trapped by the top teeth and the head clamps shut with a snap, the slicer decimates the entire creature into pulp within four seconds.

Where the necks meet is a solid, very flexible base which flaps up and down to propel the Zapro through the atmosphere. This base looks as if it is made of thick leather covered in a fine mesh, while the necks are made of overlapping plates of a compound which resembles metal, but makes the sound of plastic when hit by a catapulted ball bearing. This last fact would be another Hadrian would discover soon.

Lantar stared at the bag of crystals he had taken from the disappearing creature during the recent battle with the Dugiri. Perhaps these glittering shapes held the secret of disappearing. He would hand these over to the Omnipotence who leads the first planet ship here. They will then be sent to and investigated by Ultrasciences and the Omniscience.

If the secret of invisibility is discovered, Lantar may be updirected to Omnipotence – Mightiest Warrior! Stretching with pride and excitement, he rally-called his warriors for another raid on the Dugiri. As the Zapro army flapped towards him, he noticed SS93 taking just a little longer than he ought to have to respond to his order. 'I will pick my time: Perhaps during battle will be opportune: I must set an example to them all.' So thinking, Lantar leaned forward into streamlined position, flapped himself into flight and led his troops forward. A good raid would bring more haspira, perhaps some more crystals and the capture of Dugiri for investigation of 'live' samples.

**

Hadrian settled down with Jurgat at the mouth of the cave fissure and spread his poster on the ground.

"Where will we find the bag of crystals, Jurgat?"

"Place hand on Copernicus." Hadrian complied. "Move digit slow. Voice in head. Follow."

Hadrian slowly moved his forefinger away from the crater, moving it in increasing circles using Copernicus as the centre. He felt a distinct tingle in his finger and stopped its movement. The Words 'Lake of

Perseverence' sounded in his forehead and his moving finger left a clear outline of the feature on his poster, south east of his starting position.

"Is that it?" he asked Jurgat.

"Just a start. Continue."

Hadrian replaced his forefinger at the new location on his map and repeated his circling. After ten such tingles there was a collection of marked points from Copernicus to Zapro HQ at crater 'Alden' on the far side of the moon. Jurgat twisted three of his fronds tightly together and ran them across the poster, covering the places highlighted by Hadrian's finger. Green 'ink' flowed from the twisted fronds and traced the route they would take, making a basic map. Starting at Copernicus, the frond brush painted a route to the 'Lake of Perseverence' and on until the wrinkle ridge system of 'Dorsa Cato' was reached. At this point the brush headed due south to avoid the mountains of Mons Hansteen and Montes Cordillera.

When the location of Mons Penck was reached, the brush swept straight towards the south polar area, keeping the Lake of Excellence and the Lake of Fear to the west of his intended route. The southerly direction was maintained through small craters and features until Crater Bacon was reached. There, the brush altered course suddenly, heading east through the Lake of Solitude to the far side of the moon.

At the lake's easternmost point, Jurgat took a bearing on the ridge Dorsum Cloos and led his brush towards it, stopping soon along that line of longitude at Crater Alden. There, his brush separated into its three fronds and he floated up from the map. Hadrian marvelled at the clear, green map with the route to Zapro HQ plainly seen and all the other features clearly labelled. He studied it in silence for a short time.

"We seem to head quite far south east before altering our course to northeast and Alden, Jurgat. Is there no more direct route we could take?" Hadrian asked, analysing their journey.

"Much much Earth light Dugiri need for stamina and energy. Head south. Absorb light. Much stronger Dugiri for battle with Zapro."

As Hadrian carefully folded the map into his left hand hoodie pocket, he automatically touched the bag of ball bearings in his right pocket and the catapult in the inside breast one. Jurgat disappeared into the cave to rally his air force for their mission to Alden, Hadrian tried to absorb all that he was experiencing. His feet were itching to get on with the search for the crystals, but he couldn't help but wishing he had more time to help the Dugiri and to explore the moon at his leisure. He took two playful bounds over to the haspira pile and filled his mouth twice. He transferred his map to his jeans and loaded some of the drier haspira from the pile into the hoodie pocket. He picked up four pieces of shattered flesh to plant them alongside Darkbeast's. As he stooped he felt an inexplicable shiver run the full length of his back, from the back of his neck to the back of his heels and up again. He stood up abruptly and swivelled.

"Oh, God, no!" he exclaimed involuntarily as he gawped at Lantar, resting imperiously at the top of the crater's edge and staring down at this new strange creature. As Lantar was wondering if Hadrian was another of those creatures which could disappear, Hadrian was casting his gaze round an assortment of V-shaped beings all bobbing and weaving and obviously waiting for a command from W. 'Zapro,' he thought. He must warn the Dugiri

"Jurgat!" he bellowed. He surprised himself with the strength of his voice. One or two of the watching heads seemed to jerk up in surprise. Jurgat emerged from the cave with a swarm of following Dugiri. Hadrian bounded over to the fissure to join them, pointing up at Lantar.

"Why they do this? We give haspira to anyone who needs or asks. Zapro want destroy us and steal us. They attack Grior. Not from this moon. Why here?" Jurgat's questions were not expecting an answer. For a few moments hundreds of Dugiri flew to vital areas to attempt to defend their growing plots and cave mouth from the enemy. Hadrian decided he would be better with the part protection of the fissure and slowly pulled out his catapult. Not taking his eyes off Lantar for one moment, he worked his bag of ammunition open with his right hand without removing it from his pocket and selected one. He placed it in the sling and held it tight.

Without any apparent signal the Zapro warriors rose a few feet, adopted a twin-headed torpedo shape and started to fly in a circle round the assembled Dugiri below, like Red Indians circling a cowboy wagon train.

Lantar rose slowly, leaned forward very deliberately and lay in the atmosphere like a triple-headed javelin.

All Hell then broke loose.

CHAPTER 6

Lantar launched himself full speed for the swarm of Dugiri guarding the 'table tennis ball' plot while the Zapro warriors dive-bombed all over the place. The Dugiri went from zero mph hovering speed to upwards of 70mph in seconds like miniature berserk Ferraris. The whole area was immediately full of bangs, cracks, thuds, squelches, crunches, metallic screeches and wind whooshing as both types of creatures whizzed past, dipped, rose, swerved and clattered into each other. A Zapro torpedo headed straight for Hadrian. He was incredibly cool in these crazy circumstances. Leaning against the wall of the opening to the cave for better stability, he waited until the killer was a few metres away, one head staring at him, the other head hinged back showing a set of lethal teeth on the upper mouth and a razor sharp blade on the lower. Without hesitation, Hadrian flexed the catapult's strong rubber fully back and fired a metal ball straight in the eye of the beast. It let out a weird metallic scream and veered off to Hadrian's right and smacked into the crater wall at missile speed. Immediately, it was swarmed by scores of Dugiri pummelling its injured head and both necks. The Zapro fighter still managed to flail about and crunch a Dugiri totally, slash another three or four with its top teeth and slit another using only its lower blade. All the time the Dugiri launched themselves like mortar shells, trying to smack into the necks at the same points repeatedly.

One Dugiri smashed into the other main eye and immediately exploded, virtually blinding the warrior. It became more enraged than ever, but stumbled through the air towards the edge of the crater to leave the scene of battle. All the way it was harassed by enraged Dugiri bombs. They eventually worked a weakness in its longer neck, causing a loud crack as a panel near the head split and fell off. Zapro SS45 would take no further part in this battle and was only intent on hirpling back towards his home crater to be repaired, if possible.

Hadrian hadn't seen any of this. As soon as he heard the smack of the Zapro against the crater wall, he turned the attention of his reloaded catapult to the neck of another one and scored a direct hit on a short neck. He spent what seemed like ages simply loading and firing, loading and firing. Sometimes he would use small rocks, especially sharp ones, for ammunition and felt triumphant as he watched his accurate firing cause a gash, scrape or hole in one neck after the other. He saw Jurgat clatter into one neck just under the head and by dexterity, wonderfully-generated speed and impact over a short distance, striking the other head from an angle beyond the Zapro peripheral vision just as it opened to bare its teeth. The result was the head being knocked straight off and tumbling somersaults away in a wide parabola into the swirling dust of the arena.

The Dugiri were giving a good account of themselves but only because of their sheer weight of numbers and total disregard for their own safety when challenging a comparatively huge marauder. Many, however, were exploding on heads, necks and on the Zapro lower leathery-meshed propulsion areas and were being destroyed by versatile heads with deadly teeth. Often, the Dugiri would fire straight into one neck with a resounding plastic-sounding

'BLAM!', only to have the other head of the V pounce onto it and bite it to shreds.

Hadrian was running a little short of metal balls and retreated into the cave briefly to gather sharp rocks which he stored in his hood. It felt odd and uncomfortable but it held a good stock of catapult-sized rock chunks. He returned to his station and fired into the jungle of necks which were dodging and weaving in the mad melee that was the crater. He noticed two Zapro flying with their propulsion sacs forward and their necks stretched out behind. Their heads were hinged such that they could look under themselves as they flew. In this position they dropped onto the growing Dugiri beds and swept all the young plants before them, out of their growing solutions and onto dry and dusty areas. There seemed no purpose to their activity other than to destroy the young. Some Zapro were catching Dugiri in their teeth and then hurtling them at great speed into rocks, leaving pockets of fresh haspira everywhere.

The battle seemed to be losing its intensity as each side seemed to be running lower on energy. Some Zapro started coasting around, stuffing found haspira into the mesh area on the lower part of their bodies, like soldiers camouflaging themselves. What they were doing was gathering their spoils of war. As long as they were just mopping up haspira the Dugiri hovered wearily keeping a watch. As soon as any Zapro tried to store young plants the same way, Dugiri would attack again, if necessary crashing themselves into an area of the leathery mesh where a warrior had put small plants, destroying the captured plants immediately. There must have been twenty to thirty Zapro at the outset but at least ten had limped off damaged and one lay totally destroyed behind rocks leading to the larger plants. Hadrian decided to leave his shelter as no Zapro were coming near him. He quickly covered the ground to where the 'dead' Zapro was lying. He looked around him and all seemed abandoned here. Some of the plants had exploded, some were missing and some still grew undisturbed. The Dugiri defenders had obviously fought a magnificent action here.

'They certainly made short work of you,' he thought, as he looked carefully and close up at the slain

Zapro. He tried to absorb every detail of the lower, pouch area, the necks and the heads. This was difficult as one head had been almost totally ripped off, the other lay a short distance away and there were deep holes and slashes in the necks. 'I wonder how many Dugiri perished in this fight?' he wondered. The metallic mesh was cut in several places and leathery fronds trailed over the ground. 'How could they have managed this?'

SS93 would never be able to tell him.

Hadrian had just noticed the start of a third neck which had been bitten through. Was this dead warrior Lantar?

His head experienced radio interference and then it cleared to say, "No, beast. I am Lantar. Who are you?"

Hadrian's heart missed a beat as he leapt up to face the menace of the Zapro leader. The three heads were perched on a body only ten metres from him. Lantar was a couple of feet taller than Hadrian. He glanced left and right to see if there was any vantage point he could reach. He felt as if Lantar was reading his mind and waiting for him to move. The central head was slightly nearer him than the other two, although all eyes were on him. Hadrian's mind raced. Take middle eye out with ball bearing, bolt for cover of cave while Lantar is confused and pick off the other heads from the shelter of the fissure.

He loaded and pulled back the band just as Jurgat jetted into one of Lantar's side heads from behind, with an almighty crash. The centre head swivelled immediately so Hadrian switched his aim to the other side head and released his thunderbolt. It smacked into the outside peripheral eye, leaving a blind gouge where it had been. Lantar gave a metallic angry scream.

Then three things happened all at once. Hadrian tried to bolt for the cave but the head he had just injured speared his jeans just above the ankle and yanked him up in the air where he dangled upside down, held by the top teeth only. About fifty Dugiri hurtled themselves into all necks, head and torso setting off explosions like fireworks on the plastic/ metal neck plates. The third thing that happened was that the central mouth sprang open as far as it could and bit deeply into Jurgat. The head Jurgat had damaged had enough strength to keep the Dugiri leader pressed into the strong central mouth, while slicing at Jurgat's skin with its own lower blade.

Lantar reacted to the sudden attack by heading off at speed towards the crater's edge, Jurgat trapped, Hadrian dangling and Dugiri bombarding him from every direction. But Lantar was a mighty warrior and took all the blows that rained upon him. He decided to use a free head to attack some of the Dugiri and as both of his heads would now need repair he decided to slice through the other dangling creature to get rid of it for now. After all it could not possibly know the secret of invisibility or it would have used it by now. So the head with the main eye and the inside peripheral still working brought its teeth down to engage with its blade, while Hadrian dangled and Dugiri swarmed in to try to help.

The head and eyes on that particular neck snapped shut. The eyes were now protected and the teeth had taken their bite. Luckily for Hadrian the bite simply sliced right through his jeans and he clattered unceremoniously to the ground. He sat up dazed as Lantar continued up the terraces at the edge of Copernicus, still under attack, still slicing with one blade and crushing with the main mouth into the struggling Jurgat. Hadrian glanced at his jeans and wondered how he was going to explain them to his mother. He was already leaping up the terraced steps in pursuit. When he reached the top his heart sank like a stone. Lantar was disappearing at speed into the distance, leather sac flapping furiously and three heads as one single warhead. The head which had held Jurgat was flopping about as if badly damaged. The Dugiri were more concerned with their broken leader. Jurgat lay a sorry mess beside an outcrop of rocks. He was sliced through at least thirty times from the side head's attack. All knobbles had gone and his skin cut through at various points. Ninety per cent of his fronds were gone. The side which had been in the central mouth was totally devastated. Lantar had obviously succeeded in biting right through Jurgat, gouging a huge hole out of him. The hole covered an area of over half his total side. He lay with most of his haspira spewed out of his side but without the energy to explode himself.

"No, Jurgat, No, No, No!" shouted Hadrian as he bounded over to his friend and gently cradled him and as much of his vomited haspira as he could gather. He tried to feed the haspira back into the wound gently but knew in his heart of hearts that he was wasting his time. "Can a leader regenerate?" he asked no-one in particular, in a barren plea.

"Jurgat time has come. Not energy to explode self. Need help."

"I can't do it Jurgat, I can't kill you, I can't."

"What is 'kill'? I need help to finish my time. Pintar will help. Zapro, why they do this Hadrian?"

"I'm sorry, Jurgat, I just do not know at all."

"You defend bravely today. Dugiri friend. Find Grior bag now. Put Jurgat in rock corner. Rocks Dugiri friends."

Hadrian reluctantly placed Jurgat carefully down against two corner rocks and stepped back into the hovering crowd of Dugiri. He felt the tears starting to well up and his lip start to tremble. He took a deep breath to try and compose himself, but still he felt the silent tear run down his cheek. A nearby creature coasted towards him and used a frond to wipe the tear away. 'How can these wonderful creatures not feel pain when they have compassion?' wondered Hadrian again. As he watched, Pintar emerged from within the crater and joined his new followers. There was total silence. The Earth was rising, casting warm blue light and shadows over the scene.

Jurgat simply said, "Please now Pintar." Ten frondless Dugiri hung suspended in the frugal atmosphere until their new leader made the slightest forward rocking movement. All ten immediately plummeted into Jurgat leaving his, and their, haspira in a huge mound. After a few seconds Hadrian stepped forward, made a hammock shape at the front of his hoodie, knelt down and scooped all the haspira into it. Standing up and totally oblivious to the Dugiri round about him, he walked very deliberately towards the crater, entered it and headed for the cave. Pintar followed a few feet behind and the others glided in and around the cave behind Pintar. Hadrian went straight for the room where Pintar had been waiting for his time to be leader. He clambered in carefully and laid the heaped haspira in the centre of the room. Climbing out again, he said, "Haspira fit for a leader. Only a leader should have this haspira. Which one of these will be the next leader, Pintar?" asked Hadrian looking at five larger Dugiri, growing separately from the others in purple gel. Pintar could have told Hadrian that Dugiri did not actually need to take haspira but he decided not to. "You may choose."

Hadrian felt honoured. "Thank you Pintar. Thank you very much." He surveyed the five carefully and noticed one had a small blemish of a blue spot on its back. "That one, please, it has the Earth marked on it!" There were creatures whooshing around, somersaulting and a new thing to Hadrian – many of them zoomed past him, gently dragging a frond across his face or shoulder or leg, depending on what height they were at.

"Dugiri like choice!"

"What's its name, Pintar?"

"Name given now. Name now is 'Hadrian'."

Hadrian grinned from ear to ear as new Hadrian vibrated rapidly out of the clutches of the gel, rose in front of Hadrian and having done one forward somersault, new Hadrian drifted by old Hadrian into his grooming chamber to the usual celebrations of the flying fruits.

As they emerged into the earthlight a scene of considerable destruction faced them, but without further ado every creature started restoring damaged plant beds, replanting, gathering of haspira which had not been plundered and tidying up manageable debris. Most of the replanting was at the very start of the growing cycle and as no Zapro had gained access to the cave beds there was very little to do there.

Hadrian dragged the remains of SS93 towards the haspira heap, as Pintar had requested, saying that Darkbeast often took away parts of scrap Zapro when it visited. As Hadrian carried the separated head towards the same heap as the body, his father sprung into mind again.

"Yes, Hadrian, we will go to the moon and set up a father and son business dealing in scrap Zapros to sell to the Darkbeasties. We'll call it 'Scrapros' and make our fortune!" Hadrian shook his head and hoped that, because he'd thought of that crummy joke, he was not turning into his dad! He gathered some flesh pieces and proceeded to the planting area.

*

Lantar flew home with mixed feelings. There had been no crystals and no secret of invisibility but a very successful raid nevertheless. Casualties had been higher than he had expected. What was that beast with the Dugiri? He would have to return after his repairs and capture it. It fought well and moved like a small Deathbringer. That was it! Those Deathbringer creatures which hunt alone and destroy Zapro scouts – it was one of them. Lantar would call it 'Little Death'. Little Death moved and was shaped like a smaller version of them and he too fought by projecting things through the atmosphere. Perhaps Little Death could be made to lead Zapro to Deathbringer's crater.

Yes, Lantar must give the capture of Little Death some thought. We got plenty of haspira, though – and – he chuckled evilly to himself, whatever happened to my space soldier number 93? As Lantar flew towards home he spent the rest of the journey remembering how he had surprised SS93 behind the rock screen. It was over in no time at all. He caught him completely by surprise while he was being buzzed by Dugiri. Having grasped both necks immediately under the heads in an inescapable clamp, all that 93 could do was to thresh about as Lantar's middle mouth launched a frenzied assault on both necks and propelling pouch.

All the Dugiri zapped away and left him to get on with it! He'd even had time to indulge in a token attack on the middle neck growth when one of 93's heads snapped off suddenly, thus freeing a second head to finish off the job. He made sure two of his warriors saw what was happening. They would tell all the others and not one of them would dare to challenge his position now. He slowed his flying speed when he became within reasonable distance of Crater Alden. He wanted to make sure the others had time to spread the story before he got home. His thoughts ran with him: 'Upon my return, I may order one or two of the badly-damaged warriors to be destroyed and reconstructed using spares as a different number. I may say they failed me and our planet in battle. Perhaps – depending on how I feel. I'll need to have my eye reconstructed and some panels repaired. One side head would need replaced. My repairs would be done first.' He coasted in on a breeze of self-satisfaction as he saw the sentries announcing his imminent arrival to his cheering warriors.

*

CHAPTER 7

Tidying the crater took ages, but Hadrian marvelled at the thorough job being done by the Dugiri. His mum would have loved a few pet Dugiri for cleaning her kitchen! He even found a collection of many of his ball bearings which had been retrieved and placed in a little group at the mouth of the cave. At long last the cleaning up was complete and the crater looked as good as ever. Hadrian shambled wearily into a corner of the main cave where a bundle of leathery strips lay invitingly. Pintar breezed in and invited Hadrian to rest on the soft mattress of Zapro parts.

"Darkbeast sometime regenerate here before home goes. You use yes?"

Hadrian needed no second invitation. He definitely needed a power nap.... just a short one, then he must get the crystals. As he slept, the Dugiri flew out into dust storms and revitalised their energy levels. Some of the wounded produced a sticky substance from their fronds and knobblies and smeared it over splits and scrapes.

Hadrian had a weird dream that his mother had found Grior in his bed in the morning and decided to keep him instead of Hadrian. Dad took Grior to the football and he was made team captain, performing amazing weaving and dribbling skills on his own sphere. Everyone hero-worshipped the boy from outer space and, worst of all, Lorna seemed to *really* like him. She taught him chess and table tennis and he walked with her and Spangles every evening. Grior laughed at all Dad's jokes and no-one seemed to be noticing that Hadrian was not there. It was as if he had never existed. When he awoke, he was relieved to find that he had just been dreaming. He decided he really must tell Lorna how he felt about her when he returned to Earth, before someone else stepped in. He sat up and munched a generous handful of haspira from the supply in his pocket. Pintar hovered near the mouth of the cave. Hadrian rose, shook himself down and checked for map, catapult, ammunition and knife.

He was going to wish Pintar a good morning but had no idea if he had slept for hours or minutes and so had no idea of the correct time. He followed Pintar out into the cavern where refreshed Dugiri were patiently waiting to embark on the journey to retrieve Grior's bag.

They set off at a comfortable pace for Hadrian, heading for the Lake of Perseverence. What an appropriate name for a lake in his adventure, our hero thought. The moon's lakes were waterless but called lakes nevertheless. Now and then, Pintar would take up position to one side of Hadrian's moving head and point out a landmark or feature. As they were nearing the wrinkle ridge system called Dorsa Cato, Pintar indicated huge grey pyramids to the west and told Hadrian they were cinder cones. These were the remains of small extinct volcanoes. At the ridge the swarm diverted due south, skirting the mountains of Mons Hansteen and Montes Cordillera.

Maintaining a direction of due south they soon reached Mons Penck and skimmed up and over the barren mountain. From the top there was a splendid view to the west of the Lake of Excellence and the Lake of Fear. Pintar also pointed out from the summit a surface crack down below. It had been formed when one block of the moon's crust had slipped away from the other. The fault ran away as far as the eye could see. Hadrian amused himself and certainly caught the attention of several Dugiri by leaping into a flying crucifix shape and gliding down some parts of the descent.

On they sped towards the southernmost point of their journey, the flying fortress absorbing earthlight every inch of the way. There were several old lava rills across their path which were easily cleared. Just as their next reference point at Crater Bacon came into view, Hadrian's attention was drawn to two bright streaks of ejected rock emerging from a small crater nearby to the East.

"Those sites of meteorite impact, Hadrian. Many on both sides moon. Some old, some recent. Not many lava rills on far side. Moon crust thicker. Volcano much harder to manage push through surface."

Hadrian wondered how on earth, or rather, on the moon, Pintar knew so much. As Crater Bacon became more than a distant outline, Hadrian pulled out his map to consult with it. Incredibly, all the places, features and areas they had passed through or mentioned were clearly labelled on the poster, including the cinder cones, surface fault etc. He would take more haspira when they reached the crater although he was still feeling fine. By the time he rested on a flat rock inside Crater Bacon, the whole troupe had journeyed from approximately 10 degrees north to 50 degrees south and 20 degrees west to 20 degrees east. The crater headed round to the far side of the moon further than he could see.

"So it's east to the far end of the Lake of Solitude and then bear north again, Pintar," said Hadrian referring once more to his map and munching some haspira.

"Indeed, yes friend. Dugiri first have surprise for you! Follow Pintar, please. The flight of Dugiri sped ahead of them at Pintar's nod and disappeared with much noise from rubbing fronds into an opening in the walls. By the time Hadrian reached it, only a few seconds later, there was no visual sign of any of them. The opening was actually a tunnel leading underground and he could hear from the distant depths the sounds of whizzing and stringing of fronds. He followed Pintar along the tunnel by holding onto the back of his pilot and trusting his guide to see him safely down the sloping surface. As his eyes got used to the dark he was aware of a glow emanating from the now nearby sounds of excited Dugiri, into the passageway. Suddenly, the tunnel veered left and Hadrian was suddenly smacked in the face with lovely warm air. Not for the first time in the past few days of his life, he stood and marvelled at the scene before him.

He could only describe this as a swimming pool with dry water! He could only guess that some kind of volcanic activity rumbling away down below had heated the air in this cavern. The air escaping from the volcano had a blue-green tinge of chemicals mixed with it, almost like the chlorine in a swimming pool. The blue heated air was at a lovely temperature and Hadrian would discover that it came up to his shoulder height in depth, around the cave walls. Twice his height was left in headroom above the 'swimming' air. The Dugiri were having a ball. Diving into the mix and forward-flipping to the far end of the cavern was a great favourite. Groups of synchronised creatures were doing little routines in the blue, while others were hovering like the Red Arrows display team and then diving in formation into the welcoming swirls. They were swimming in the suspension by somersaulting, back flipping, rotating like propellers and some were travelling like bouncing bombs. A group of leaping red fruit dolphins played alongside him.

This was incredible. Hadrian wondered yet again how these wonderful beings could feel pleasure and emotion, yet not experience pain. Perhaps pain had been edited from their nervous systems to enable them to fulfil their apparent purpose of smashing themselves into smithereens to produce haspira. That seemed like a reasonable theory to Hadrian as he decided the swimming gas looked too good to miss out on. He leaned forward and swept his hands, breast-stroke style through the warm, dense gases and had to prevent himself falling forward into a floating position. He slipped off his hoodie, T-shirt, trainers jeans and socks and strode into the mix. Hopping up, he adopted the front crawl position and completed a leisurely length of the cave. He tumble-turned and came back, alternating front and back crawl strokes. This was fantastic. He tumbled, paddled and swam, joining in the fun and frolics. All too soon, Pintar signalled for time and the Dugiri emerged from the warm, coloured mist to continue their quest. Hadrian dressed quickly and laid his right hand on Pintar's back in order to wend his way up the dark tunnel to the surface.

"That was wonderful, Pintar. Why don't you live here all the time?"

"Growing conditions not so good. Better Copernicus."

The journey to the surface did not seem as long as

when going downwards to the underground swimming grotto. As Hadrian emerged from the split in the cavern wall, the Dugiri were already hovering purposefully, ready to be on their way towards the far side of the moon and, hopefully, the Universe Bag.

Hadrian bounded along at a comfortable pace using the swarm as his navigators. The vast lake was pretty featureless and flat and made for easy progress. Every now and then they would meet a small dust 'disturbance' – too gentle to be called a storm – and a handful of Dugiri would deviate from the flightpath to act as vacuum cleaners, making quick work hoovering the entire wispy clouds without the main body of troops altering speed. As they travelled, Hadrian carried out a 'touch' check that he still had his catapult and metal balls and his knife. He was becoming increasingly focused on the task ahead. His head was swimming with questions and concerns.

If they found the Zapro crater would the bag be there? Would they be able to retrieve it? How many Zapro would be there? Hadrian couldn't see Pintar but sent him a mind message. 'Have we a plan of attack, Pintar?"

Almost immediately the reply came, "Stop to plan at rock circle soon. Hadrian help make plan too. Not long."

In the waning sun's rays Hadrian made out the silhouettes of a group of rocky hillocks. If they were arranged in a circle these could be where they were going to sort out battle tactics. Hadrian felt a strange mix of apprehension and excitement welling up inside him as he increased his speed towards the shadowy peaks. The advancing army soon reached the circle of rocks and rested up.

Hadrian spread out his map. A ridge bearing the name of Dorsum Cloos was situated at 1 degree N and about 90 degrees E. Hadrian wondered who had named all these places. Dorsum Cloos sounded more like a German footballer than a ridge of rock and rubble. He placed his finger on the ridge but felt no sharp pain. He swallowed a handful of haspira and looked around. Yet again he could only marvel at the sight he was beholding. With the exception of Pintar, the Dugiri were circling gently in an anti-clockwise direction about ten feet above ground level. It was like watching a huge fairground carousel of red pods freewheeling to draw the attention of people to the availability of the attraction. The difference was the almost total silence which prevailed. Pintar was resting on a cushion of air at Hadrian's elbow. Sunshine glinted weakly on the circling group giving the brief impression of flickering flames at random points on the circle.

Hadrian ran his finger from Dorsum Cloos to where he thought they were roughly situated. Somewhere along that line lay the Zapro warriors, licking their wounds and planning more violence, thought Hadrian. His finger lazily moved a little further east and started to tingle slightly. He moved it further in the same direction and almost immediately felt a much more pronounced stab. Examining the map, he noticed the faint outline of a circle of peaks where he felt the stab.

'We must be here!' he thought. Starting from this new point, Hadrian ran his finger up the poster in a straight line towards Dorsum Cloos. He had scarcely made much progress when he felt a distinct jab. It was very strong and Hadrian knew it was the end of his search. He read off 'Crater Alden' and immediately knew it was where they would find Zapro HQ.

"Plan now can do," said Pintar. Hadrian was delighted he had pinpointed the HQ crater, but when he glanced towards Pintar, he noticed that the leader had in fact moved away from his elbow and was giving his attention to a space which had opened up in the circling mass. The circle was now static and hovering. Pintar's comments had nothing to do with Hadrian. Almost at the moment that Hadrian noticed the gap in the ring, four Dugiri came through the space at a phenomenal speed and whizzed to a dead stop at arm's length in front of Pintar.

"Excellent, scouts. All four safe. Excellent. Report now."

Hadrian watched in wonder as one scout jerked round in a horizontal circle in front of his leader, stopping briefly to send 'squeak' messages with two or three fronds. As this was happening, scout two was carrying out a similar pattern of reporting in a vertical circle. Scout three was similarly spilling information using an aerial circle turning diagonally at 45 degrees to the horizontal, being high on the left as Pintar watched and low on the right. The final scout was mirroring scout three's movement, rotating high on the right and low on the left. It was somewhat like watching the puzzle that was on Dad's office at work, thought Hadrian, where a gyroscope had four circles all moving in odd ways at once. When the scouts finished, Pintar wheeled round to Hadrian.

"Good news if Dugiri quick. Zapro crater at Alden. Hadrian know this. Warriors being repaired. Lantar having much repair. Crystal bag in large machine with much haspira. Machine sending space message out. Why? More Zapro coming? Destroy message sender, Hadrian. No more Zapro here."

"Would we have to get into the machine to destroy it or could I use my catapult?" Hadrian held up his catapult as if to help with his question. "If Dugiri could distract them I could destroy the message sender and get the crystals. Do you want the haspira?"

"Haspira not needed. Good idea. Dugiri make chaos. Hadrian disable space bleeper. Grior's bag saved. Scouts report small robots repairing Zapro. Destroy these robots and immobilise Zapro for all time."

This idea obviously went down a treat with the Dugiri, according to the twirls and flips, the rolls and squeaks. Hadrian was ready for further discussion when he realised that the whole lot had already started off for Crater Alden. Hadrian wished the last of the sunlight would disappear, but it was clinging on as if reluctant to go to bed and miss the anticipated battle. Hadrian's head was buzzing again. If all went well he would soon be returning the Universe Bag to Grior. What if all did not go well? Hadrian hadn't given that possibility much thought but then he hadn't anticipated encountering Zapro. He glanced down at the v-shaped chunk out of his jeans. He still hadn't worked out how he was going to explain it to his mother. 'Ha!' he laughed, 'I might have a lot more explaining to do than just that!' He wished he'd told Grior just to appear in his bedroom and he could have left a note for his parents to explain the whole thing. Even if they didn't see the note, Grior would be there and could fix scramblers to them. He had been in too much of a selfish hurry at the thought of the excitement of the adventure.

'So let's get it done!' he chided himself.

The Dugiri dipped as one and swept along like a huge hovercraft just above the surface. Hadrian crouched and tried to move in a lower trajectory to emulate the Dugiri. They must be getting close. The light was going fast. The swarm slowed as if waiting for the light to die before it made its final push for victory. Everything was deadly quiet in the Dugiri camp as they slowed to a glide and Hadrian to a jog. A cloak of darkness swam over them and almost in compensation for the reduction in effectiveness of eyesight , his ears picked up distant sounds emanating from the crater a football pitch length ahead. The crater could be seen in part because little hazy glows of pale light flitted above its surface. The Dugiri slowed to crawling pace. For the first ever time Hadrian was moving slightly faster than his hosts. He withdrew his catapult and gave it a few experimental tugs.

He had noticed in the recent battle that the ball bearings travelled like bullets in this atmosphere. This would be very helpful. He made his way forward through the Dugiri. They were all here helping him. Perhaps if he could help destroy the tiny robots and immobilise the transmitter that would in some way help repay their friendship and support. He was just behind Pintar. Hadrian crouched and moved slowly, slowly over the last few metres. There appeared to be no sentries but then Zapro's HQ had never been attacked before. In fact, it would not have occurred to Lantar that the Dugiri were capable of launching an attack on him. If only he knew that, as the last bits of solder were being laser-burned onto the optic circuit of his replacement eye, the whole scene was being surveyed by hundreds of patient Dugiri and one young Deathbringer.

He would soon be very aware of their presence.

*

CHAPTER 8

Hadrian drank in the scene below. He could see now that the robots were the source of the lights, from a sort of banana-shaped torch atop their frames. There seemed to be four of them busy doing various repairs to different warriors and a fifth which was doubling up with one of the others to work on Lantar. It lay with one head flopped to the side while one robot seemed to be working on the replacement eye and the other on his neck and lower body area damage. There seemed to be remarkably few Zapro about. Hadrian counted 35. Where were the others? He expected twice that number, or more. Perhaps some were in caves and niches out of sight. He would just have to keep watching to see if any more emerged from anywhere. Bits of Zapro lay about all over the place like a scrap metal yard, but the robots were rummaging in amongst them, selecting bits to use for rebuilding and repairs.

He had a good view of the robot working on Lantar's eye. It was about three feet tall and resembled a mobile mini hat stand. Caterpillar tracks formed its base and eight arms hung like branches from various points at different heights on the central pole. The arms had a variety of hand attachments, two with mechanical clamps, one with a bundle of screwdriver-type attachments and one with three or four lever attachments on it. Hadrian was trying to see the other arms when his attention was drawn to another robot using an arm with a crimper on it.

This crimper was heat-sealing rips in the leathery part of the damaged Zapro's torso. A smell of hot leather rose from crimpers doing such work. The robot then brought another arm into play which sewed lengths of wire in a criss-cross direction, repairing the mesh 'basket'. The other two arms had expandable grips, the type which a human could use for tightening and unscrewing lids of jars of varying sizes. Each robot was topped by a swivelling, crescent-shaped light.

They should be easy to topple. He glanced at nearby Pintar and whispered, "The robots, Pintar. Knock them over and blast Dugiri into the space between their wheels and caterpillar tracks. Explode in the gap and the haspira will clog up their means of movement. If they can't move we can finish them off later. I can't see the machine, though."

"Dugiri see to robots. Also smash lights. Will totally destroy later. Machine in opening behind Lantar. Can see just from over here."

Hadrian ducked behind the crater edge and moved

over to Pintar. His eyes took a few moments to focus in but soon saw the machine. It seemed to him it was a spaceship of some kind. He could see red and yellow lights blinking rapidly on and off alternately. A high-pitched whine was also coming from the machine. The transmitter! Had the Zapro crash-landed on the moon and were sending out distress signals? That didn't matter for now. It had to be disabled or destroyed.

He was sure he could hit it from where he was. He only saw the crystals when a robot moved towards the spaceship to pick up a segment of neck for refitting. Its rotating beam briefly picked up the beautiful kaleidoscope of colour each time it swept round like a lighthouse beam. Hadrian gasped at the beauty of Grior's bag.

"Pintar, let me try to hit the transmitter from here. If we disable it, it might cause a distraction if the Zapro think it has broken down. If their attention is on the machine we can creep nearer and spring an attack. I may be able to reach the bag."

"Good. Hadrian get bag. Go to Grior soon as possible. Dugiri continue fight. Good luck."

It hadn't occurred to Hadrian that, in the midst of battle, he would bite the Earth crystal and simply disappear from the scene without saying goodbye to his friends. The reality of the moment sank in.

"Thank you, Pintar. Thank you, thank Jurgat, thank Dugiri."

Pintar rubbed his rough shell gently against

Hadrian's heart and stroked his face with six long, caressing fronds; "Make good shot, Hadrian."

Hadrian turned with regret and also anger mounting inside him. He withdrew two ball bearings from his pocket, putting one into the sling and laying the other beside him. He settled comfortably into a prone firing position and settled his breathing.

Lantar was happy with his new eye system and repairs done to his necks. His lower pouch needed minor attention and a head still to be replaced. He grinned slyly in his head. It had been a splendid idea to return to his crater from the recent skirmish venting fake rage on his cheering troops. Showing the battle damage he had sustained as being the result of their cowardice, he had selected twelve soldiers for instant dismantling by the robots. He had also generated a fake rant at all of them for not coming to help him deal with the traitor SS93 who had refused to fight. He rounded on the two soldiers he had made sure had seen him destroy 93 and publicly blamed them for lack of commitment to him. They were dispatched for circuit replacement. Having been immobilised by the robots, removing their entire operational circuits, the two warriors were placed on display. Lantar would have the robots replace the exact same circuits after a while. The two warriors would then return to an army with a loyalty maintained through fear. Lantar lay back and ordered two robots to replace the damaged head. As he stretched out he was aware that he felt that something was not quite as it should be.

He sat up, looked around, up and down but couldn't see anything amiss. He suddenly realised that it was a sound that was missing. The beacon had stopped transmitting!

Hadrian's breathing soon settled down and a cold calmness overrode his emotions. He took very careful aim between the two blinking lights. He had no idea where the transmitter was situated but this would do for starters. The Dugiri hung silently suspended from sight behind the crater rim. He steadied his aim, extended the catapult to its utter limit and released his bullet with a soft sigh of relaxing rubber. Seconds later there was a sharp crack which was lost to the Zapro in all the noise of repairs being done. Thinking he had missed, Hadrian reloaded. It was Pintar who said, "Hadrian. Bleeping stopped."

Flushed with his success, he took aim for the yellow light. As he released his second round he noticed Lantar jerking up into a non-prone position. His aim was fantastically accurate and the yellow light exploded loudly followed by the red one in quick succession. A fire sparked into immediate life as the first robots reached the craft and started to tackle it, trying to dismantle damaged bits. They seemed to be oblivious to the flames, but the electrics were sparking, exploding in a series of bangs and oozing thick, narrow plumes of black smoke. The first wave of Dugiri had smashed over the two immobilised warriors, toppled two robots and were peppering as many necks and torsos as possible before any Zapro, including Lantar, realised they were being attacked. It flashed through Lantar's mind that it perhaps wasn't so clever to have disabled so many of his warriors, as he was pummelled by missile Dugiri and was scrunching one he caught on flypast.

Hadrian scrambled downwards and along the dark perimeter as the chaotic frenzy developed. The odds were much better for the Dugiri than at the Copernicus raid and the element of surprise had been wonderful, but the Zapro were getting into their stride now, fighting with the strength gained from real fear of failure and its consequences. The robots were useless. They tried to help their cause by waving and swiping with all of their arms but lack of speedy mobility and the sheer weight of force of hurtling Dugiri meant that they were all soon knocked over and totally clogged up with haspira. Lantar was fighting like a demon possessed. Despite one useless flopping head he was fighting with the fury of a leader who is terrified that his whole expedition is falling apart. He had seen some of the robots go down. Without them there could be no repairs. The transmitter was burning and he had been caught out by the attack. His superiors would parade him in disgrace then propel him into outer space in an Ejection Bubble. He would drift in space until his Bubble was hit by rocks or attacked and he would be destroyed.

He would recover! They would only need one working robot. The robot could fix some of the other robots. They could then repair Zapro and his leaders would never know. These desperate thoughts filled his deluded programmer as he bit, swung, sliced, spat out rocks, rammed Dugiri torso-first and even used his flopping head with the teeth and blade exposed for the occasional 'lucky' shot. As battle raged on, Pintar estimated that about a third of his army had been destroyed or self-destructed. He could see Hadrian trying to edge his way round towards the smouldering machine but he still had some way to go. He swivelled at the sound of a Zapro zapping at him torso first. Pintar generated instant speed and smacked the Zapro head on. Both fighters were deflected off course and immediately started seeking another target.

Hadrian was getting there. The Dugiri were doing a magnificent job in totally occupying the warriors and the shadowy rocks were doing the rest. So far so good. From the safety of darkness he had fired off several catapult shots at necks and eyes with about 70% success. He was beginning to pass behind the area where Lantar had been lying. The Spaceship was only ten steps away.

Hadrian decided he could make a run for it. One minute or so from now I could be back on Earth, he thought. He took one last sweeping glance around at the noise and clamour of fierce battle, crouched into a sprint position and saw it. He wasn't sure at first, it was so dark over at the smoking craft. Then there was no doubt about it. Loping away clutching the bag of crystals was one of the Darkbeast creatures. This one was not friendly like the one which helped the Dugiri.

It was spotted by one Zapro as it scaled the rock ledges. Hadrian was still reminded of the gorillas in the film 'Planet of the Apes' when he watched them move. His opinion was reinforced when the nearest Zapro neck lunged towards it and it produced a heavy weapon like a short-handled pick axe and drove it straight through the head and deep into the mouth. The weapon stuck fast. Hadrian's eyes widened. 'Getting that out will be like removing the sword in "The Sword and the Stone"'. The ear-splitting metallic scream which came from the warrior followed it as it disengaged from Darkbeast and staggered off in a zigzag to try to regroup. Whether it was that sound or a glint from the bag of crystals, the eyes on Lantar's wounded head saw the creature. Hadrian had never picked up any Zapro language through his scrambler, but he certainly picked up Lantar's hysterical roar. As Dugiri hit him repeatedly and the other two heads snapped and splattered his enemy, the redundant mouth screamed;

"DEATHBRINGER! I WILL DESTROY YOU! ALL OF YOU!"

Lantar tried to shake off his formation of attacking missiles and buzzing bombers. Despite extensive damage to his injured neck and very visible cracks and splits on the other two, Lantar drove himself towards the spot where Deathbringer had disappeared from sight. He was moving relatively slowly, seeking out any hiding place. From his secure shadow Hadrian fired at Lantar's lolling eye and immediately blinded it.

Lantar felt the sting: the same sting as he had got from Little Death's weapon. So all Deathbringers have these weapons after all he thought. I will find this one which has taken the crystals and totally destroy it.

The crystals may save me being bubbled into space. As he struggled to rid himself of Dugiri attackers he flapped doggedly up and over the edge of the crater. The Dugiri lost interest in him as he was leaving and returned to add their weight to the battle.

As soon as he disappeared, Hadrian realised that if he was to retrieve the crystals he too would need to face Deathbringer. It seemed the best way to achieve that would be to track Lantar as he trailed Deathbringer. If he was lucky, the two of them would fight each other and he could get his hands on the Bag long enough to get home. He took two steps forward and came tumbling down as an immobilised robot clamped his leg with the one arm it had remaining. Hadrian yelped in pain as his calf started to constrict. He fired his catapult at point blank range into the robot's light source. The crescent-shaped light emitting area smashed completely and the light vanished. The grip lessened slightly, but still held. Thinking quickly, Hadrian dragged himself and the clinging robot towards its other broken arms. Selecting the one with levers, he picked it up and tried to prise open the clamp with them. Nothing moved. He used the amputated arm to thresh at the place where the arm gripping him was attached to the central structure, without result. The clamp was causing severe pain to

Hadrian but he guessed he was lucky that the robot was damaged and not able to exert maximum force into its grip. He looked around frantically for something to help him. He dragged himself and his attached problem into a slight undercut niche in the rock wall. This should keep him free from Zapro and their vicious teeth. He tried twisting the main body but that just intensified the pain. Where was the power unit operating this thing? It could only be in the disc area housing the lights.

Hadrian swivelled the top towards him, lifted a heavy rock and smashed it down on the disc with all his might. It splintered into thousands of shards of different materials but there was no sign of any power pack or circuit. He sifted through some of the dross for a micro-chip but there was nothing to be found and the grip was still on fast. He looked around for inspiration. As he did, he noticed Pintar fighting courageously in the heat of battle. First, the Dugiri leader appeared from nowhere at unimaginable speed to slam into the neck of a battling warrior. He hit a spot just below the head where previous damage had been inflicted by other flying torpedos. The impact sounded like a dynamite explosion and the head flew off the snapped neck to land some 40 metres away. The next manoeuvre followed immediately. A Dugiri was flying at great speed towards the watching eyes of SS61. The warrior could not believe his luck. When the Dugiri was almost upon him he snapped open his mouth to its widest possible position ready to decimate his enemy. Just as the Dugiri was about to disappear into the chasm, he stopped dead, from 60 to 0 in a split second. At that very second, with the Dugiri poised at the mouth and before SS61 had time to react, Pintar dived out of the sky at jet speed and completely smashed the head off its hinges and on to the ground. The pain in Hadrian's leg drew his attention back again. He had an idea which might work. Examining the robot's body pole, he could see inside at some of the points where other arms had been taken clean off by Dugiri, leaving holes that were roughly circular. He could see something like twisted cables passing through the pole from the lights at the top to the base tracks. Or was it the other way around? Perhaps these cables were feeding power to the clamp. He rummaged out his Swiss Army knife and prepared to gouge inside the pole when a sixth sense stopped him. What if the core was electrified and live? He reached a strip of leathery skin lying round waiting to be used in repair work and wrapped it round the handle of the knife. Protected from electric current, he plunged the largest blade into the nearest hole. Smoke emerged and a horrible smell of burning flesh escaped.

Hadrian wriggled the blade back and forth. He had made some difference but not enough to destroy the innards. He withdrew the knife, refolded the blade and pulled out the saw blade. Having wrapped the skin round the haft again, he plunged in and started sawing. He soon heard the sinewy rope snap and the grip on his leg loosened completely and the arm fell loose. He rubbed and massaged his calf briefly. 'Right,' he thought, 'Now for Deathbringer.' He stood up quickly and felt the almighty blow to the top of his head. He had seen cartoon drawings of characters receiving blows to the head and seeing stars. He now knew it was true. As the firework sparkler burst in his head and a circle of stars spun round, he completely lost consciousness.

*

CHAPTER 9

Thud! Thud! Thud! went the monotonous tune in Hadrian's head as it took the first steps towards clearing itself. There was a sharp pain on the very crown of his head and a ringing in his ears. A dull pain curtained each eye and his tongue was dry. His mouth moaned and his brain connected with the sound. He rose gradually from the depths of complete unconsciousness to the surface of awareness. Thud, thud, it went on as Hadrian found his thoughts starting to reshape and his memory kicking in. The robot! He remembered now he had freed himself from it. Something had dealt him a severe and painful blow to the top of the head. No wonder it was very sore. Keeping his eyes closed he gingerly felt the stickiness on the top of his hair and he knew his head was or had been bleeding. His tongue was terribly dry. He scooped the last of his haspira into his mouth and felt lovely moisture return to his tongue and lips. The ringing in his ears faded and the thudding lessened inside his temple. He opened his eyes reluctantly to see what had hit him. If he hadn't been in so much pain he would have laughed aloud. As it was he was glad no-one had witnessed him being knocked out. He had forgotten that he had crawled under an overhang of rock while wrestling to remove the robot clamp. When he had stood up quickly, once he had freed himself, he had clattered his head on the underside of the protruding shelf of solid rock. The rest, as they say, is history.

He rolled clear of the wall and stared at the silent scene of carnage everywhere. He couldn't be certain, but it looked as if all of the Zapro had been damaged beyond repair. Heads, bits of neck, broken racks of teeth, neck plates, mesh, Zapro leather and gouged V shapes were strewn the length and breadth of the small crater. There was a profusion of haspira clumps randomly distributed over the crater floor and destroyed Dugiri lay like an extensive dead red carpet.

All of the robots were smashed into several pieces. He walked among the destroyed armies and broken machinery. The spaceship was totally burnt out and small flames flickered at various points of the melted fuselage. The Dugiri had finished off the transmitter permanently. It lay like a thousand piece jigsaw scattered on the floor. Hadrian walked over to a few haspira bundles and pocketed them as he wandered aimlessly over the battlefield. There was no sign of Pintar and no huge heap of haspira which was likely to be his remains. Nor were there any W-shaped Zapro.

Then Hadrian remembered that Lantar had headed off after the Deathbringer. He would have to go after them for the crystals. He wondered how long he had been unconscious and how much of a start Lantar had on him. He looked around for any extra weapons he could take. All that Hadrian could think of was to take a set of nine undamaged teeth which had been knocked out of a warrior's mouth. He struck the first two and the last two off the 'jawbone' and used these flattened areas to bind the tooth set onto a discarded robot's pole. He did this by bandaging the pole tightly to the flat areas of the tooth band with strips of Zapro leather fronds. He selected the only pole that had part of its light beam attachment intact in case he needed torchlight, albeit weak, to help him track Lantar.

Hadrian strode up the side of the crater, still feeling a painful tightness in the calf which had been clamped and a piercing ache where he had struck his head. At the top he looked all around looking for an indication of Lantar's trail. He leaned his weapon against the rock and took out his map. He tried to remember where the Deathbringer had dashed out of the crater and the route up the side Lantar had followed. Holding the map facing in roughly the anticipated direction, Hadrian ran his fingers in a fan shape pattern all over the sheet without feeling the merest hint of a tingle.

He turned clockwise a little to a new position and repeated the procedure; he was facing back over Crater Alden's battlefield. He smoothed his fingers over the open map and got a definite zing at a point near to 50 degrees S and 100 degrees E. He picked up his lighted rod close to the map and concentrated on the exact spot on the poster. The dim light was enough to highlight that the point was called Crater Anuchin. If the map's magic was still working as it had done so far, then Crater Anuchin should be the home of the Deathbringers. So be it, thought Hadrian, pocketing the map, touch-checking his pockets and casting a glance at his improvised weapon. He walked a little stiffly straight across the scene of carnage, rising out of the other side of Zapro HQ at a shallow point in the side. One final check of his haspira store and he set off loping as well as he could manage, towards what he hoped would be the home of the Deathbringers. His calf was hindering him with the acute pain coming from it, despite using his robot pole as a kind of walking stick . He tried manfully to put all pain from his mind and concentrate on following the correct course, keeping a watch out for any sign of Lantar or a Deathbringer. If Darkbeast was in the crater, would it help Hadrian or join the other Deathbringers in fighting him and Lantar? Hadrian felt that an ally would be very welcome in his current situation.

*

Pintar reflected as his bedraggled army wound its way home. About three quarters of the Dugiri had been destroyed along with Hadrian. At least they had destroyed all the Zapro warriors except their leader. The bleeping machine was dead. The robots had incurred the wrath of a furious mob of Dugiri, which had included Pintar, because of Hadrian's destruction. When they saw him lying destroyed, the mob launched a final frenzied attack on the pieces of robots and totally annihilated every bit of them. There was no sign of the bag of crystals. Could Hadrian have managed to get them to Grior before he himself was immobilised? He had been a brave Earth boy. No Dugiri had ever experienced a battle like that before. Perhaps they would be left in peace now. Pintar hoped so.

Hadrian was surrounded by a cloak of total silence which made his breathing sound like a mini gale blowing every time he breathed out. He wasn't tired but still found the pains in his leg and head persistently annoying, preventing him going flat out in his pursuit of the crystals. As long as the terrain was flat he could make reasonable progress, but if he landed awkwardly, the clamped leg felt as if the robot arm was still attached. There was a throbbing lump on the top of his head and a driving force in his mind. With utter determination he cast the pain out of his thoughts and redoubled his efforts.

He couldn't be bothered looking at his poster for the names of ridges or lakes as he progressed, but now and then he would open it out and use the sting from the map to make any minor adjustments to the direction he was taking towards Anuchin.

He couldn't see anything, but his ears picked up harsh sounds coming from somewhere ahead. Excitement stirred within him and Hadrian increased his stride considerably, calf or no calf. He was gaining on the source of the sounds but could still not see anything. He allowed himself to slow to a dead halt and strained to listen and see what was going on. He proceeded cautiously. The noise was definitely a disturbance of some kind. It was coming from just beyond the ridge ahead. Could this be the very crater he sought? The strength of sharp tingle on the map confirmed his hopes and by the sound of it, Lantar had found Anuchin, too. Hadrian edged forward and slowly ascended the ridge. As he reached the top, he looked for a spot where there was good shadow cover and lay flat, his head taking in the scene below hidden from view in the deep shadows.

Lantar was circling round the figure of a lone Deathbringer, making odd mechanical sounds and metallic shrieks as he moved. 'Where were the others?' wondered Hadrian, having a quick glance around. Perhaps the map was identifying where he would find the crystals. The Deathbringer pivoted slightly to ensure that it was face on to the circling Lantar at all times. The scene reminded Hadrian of a story he had read about a mongoose which had circled and bobbed and weaved until it had hypnotised a deadly snake. Lantar's hypnotic slow circling included his two functioning heads darting forward in testing lunges, keeping the

Deathbringer fully alert.

The creature was stabbing back at the probing heads with a weapon which resembled a heavy, two-handed sword without the wrist cross piece. The Deathbringer held it in its right arm. There were five poles stuck in the ground by the Deathbringer's right shoulder. Without taking his attention from Lantar, the huge gorilla shape scooped a net off the ground into its left paw. The two continued in this deadly dance, each seeking a chink in the other's defences, before launching an all-out attack. The Deathbringer looked like a Roman gladiator, with sword and net.

Lantar was showing clear signs of battle. His one side head still flapped uselessly from a neck which had been bombarded to the extent that it was bent over near the top. It was like one of those plastic straws with a concertina section so you can bend it over to drink more comfortably from the container. The other side head was cracked above the outside peripheral eye and green liquid was bubbling from the eye in a sticky drip onto the neck. Both strong necks were split at various locations, with a couple of panels swinging loose from the central one. Lantar's lower sac had been punctured in several places, with trailing leathery strands squeezing from the mesh. Bits of the strands were breaking off and littering the crater floor.

Deathbringer shifted the sword to join the net in its left paw. It pulled one of the stakes from the ground and held it up spear-like. Lantar and Deathbringer were five metres apart. Without warning, the spear jetted towards Lantar's pouch and buried itself two thirds of its length into the leather. By the time it hit, another was following in its path. The second one actually sheared off some of the mesh and ripped the leather.

Lantar rose with a screech and came straight for Deathbringer. The initial clash would have wakened the dead. As Deathbringer swiped the sword at one head, the other neck battered the creature off balance and it fell onto its own net. As the central head opened wide and dived, Deathbringer rolled away as quick as a flash and vicious jaws snapped at an arm, shearing off part of the plate just above the elbow. The gorilla leapt to its feet, but no longer had a grip on the net. It yanked another spear out of the ground and held it underhand, stabbing out at the attacking neck and heads. There was a spell of nip and tuck, with Lantar snapping and swinging and Deathbringer slashing, prodding and jumping about.

The clack and clash of neck on arms and body filled the air with angry noise as the two fierce combatants went at it hammer and tongs. Hadrian was amazed at the energy being shown by Darkbeast and the ability of Lantar to use both heads independently at high speed. Once or twice, Lantar pulled back some five or six metres as if surprised by the ability being shown by a worthy adversary. On one such occasion, Deathbringer grabbed the net again and started swinging it round in huge wide sweeps. As Lantar darted forward the net was released in a huge fan shape which smacked him full in the damaged neck. It wrapped itself round and round the bent neck and hanging head until they were totally entangled. A better result for Deathbringer would have been to have done that to one of the other heads but at least dragging the weight of the mesh slowed Lantar down noticeably.

The remaining spears were plunged into Lantar's sac. Leathery lumps leaked from the pouch and fell onto the floor. The more material that came out the less height Lantar could manage when he sprang up. It was like a boxing match, where one fighter was going for body punches to weaken his opponent, while the other was looking for one knock-out punch to finish it off. Deathbringer was gradually moving in towards the centre of the crater. Lantar probably wouldn't even notice as the two fought feverishly, teeth shaving shards of Deathbringer's skin and his flashing central mouth snapping chunks out of the panels covering Deathbringer's outer covering. So much for it being a gorilla, thought Hadrian, there was no blood coming from the open holes in the damaged arm

The more Deathbringer enticed Lantar into centre ground, the more stuffing spilled from its pouch and the less it could leap. Lantar was so full of rage he didn't notice at all. A desperate and violent lunge towards the enemy saw Lantar knock Deathbringer totally off balance with his outside neck. As it fell heavily, it smacked the open central head with the flat of its sword.

Teeth and part of the jaw blade splintered with a resounding crash and tinkle. Lantar reeled away and stopped fully ten metres away to take stock. Deathbringer cracked its head as it fell. Two panels split at their join and it staggered up with the two panels flapping up and down like a double gate in its head. Looking at them, Hadrian knew the end was near. He didn't know which, if either, he wanted to win.

Lantar coasted in for one last effort. He could see the extensive damage he had inflicted on Deathbringer but could also feel his own power of functioning fading.

His forlorn dreams of glory flashed before him. Now it was not about fame, it was about survival. Deathbringer raised itself groggily, knowing it couldn't take much more of this. Energy levels were running on empty and strength disappearing fast.

Lantar moved slowly towards his waiting enemy. His sac dragged across the moon's surface now as he struggled to remain airborne. The trailing mesh seemed to have increased one hundredfold in weight. He would make one last lunge for the head and bite it off. If his suspicions were correct, Deathbringer's circuits were all in its head. By removing the head he would destroy the beast. His central neck would attack first as a decoy with the side head going for the beast's head immediately after.

Deathbringer watched as Lantar limped directly towards it. No circling now, no leaping, just two exhausted warriors. It had only one head to worry about now. If it could smash that the fight would be over. What would it do if it was Lantar? It would probably lead with the damaged neck to distract from the able head attacking. I will ignore whatever the central neck does and go for the other head. It picked up a rock and hurled it at the advancing warrior, splitting a few more teeth and lodging in the head. It took up its sword.

With a deathly shriek, Lantar launched forward and struck Deathbringer on its chest with the very rock that was lodged in its head. The impact knocked Deathbringer's plans for six as it was batted back ten metres and its own impetus rolled it back another ten, coming to rest with a thud directly below Hadrian. Its sword lay behind the advancing Lantar. Using the wall to force itself painfully upwards, it saw that the head which had struck him was lying on the ground and the centre neck was trailing like a lizard's tail. Lantar drunkenly inched towards Deathbringer. Too winded and exhausted, it could only watch as a neck and snarling head dragged Lantar towards its position against the rocks.

Deathbringer leaned back against the rock, summoning up its last shadows of energy. As the head descended, mouth agape, It dived to the side and rolled away. Stumbling to its feet it teetered towards the sword. Lantar's mouth crashed into the rock face, biting off a considerable amount of rubble. As the mouth gouged in, Hadrian was looking straight down at the head. His catapult released a silent bullet which shot the main eye to pieces. Lantar screamed as it turned, catching Deathbringer in its peripheral vision. Dragging itself after it, Lantar was shedding the last remnants of its leather stuffing.

Deathbringer reached the sword, but could not even pick it up due to total exhaustion. Instead, it turned to face its fate, lost consciousness and crashed to the ground. Lantar was only a few metres away. It sensed the kill. It moved in for the final bite. At least, that's what its control circuit told it to do. However, when your sac has just shed the last of the leather, you cannot move. With a blood-curdling wail of exasperation it flopped menacingly towards the senseless beast, landing the length of a school ruler from its head. Its peripheral eye saw Hadrian just as he swiftly sawed off the head, terminating Lantar's existence.

*

CHAPTER 10

Hadrian kicked the dismembered head and sent a sharp pain through his calf. He winced. Cautiously, he approached the body of Deathbringer. He stood watching for any sign of life but could not see any. He gingerly lifted one limp arm. It was heavy; a dead weight. He let it drop. It gave a dull thud as it hit the ground and raised a little dust swirl. There was nothing to be done here, thought Hadrian, he must now find the crystals.

He looked around seeking clues. He tried his map again but it gave no more specific indication of the whereabouts of the crystals. The signal was sharp in the crater but the only other slight tingle came from Crater Copernicus. He moved without caution towards the rocky walls and crevices of Anuchin. This could take some time, he thought, wondering just where to start. Apart from the crater walls there were two groups of rock hills inside it. He would work along the side as far as a steep dip in it. At that point he would cross to the nearer group of rock hills and investigate that. If he still had not found the Bag by then, he would examine the other cluster and then resume from the dip in the wall. He would complete the entire circumference of the crater if necessary, although he hoped it would not be.

Loping easily over to the wall, he jammed his makeshift weapon in a crack. This would let him know when he had arrived back at the point where he started. Using his Swiss knife he worked the light disc free from the robot part and carried his torch with him into the first opening. He would only have to try caves which were large enough at the mouth for a bulky Deathbringer to get through. Had it been the smaller Dugiri who had hidden the Bag his task would have been much harder. He was making good time and soon reached halfway to the dip in the side wall. At this point, as he emerged from his sixth shallow crevice, he saw a wide split beckoning him in to a large cave. This looked more promising and Hadrian quickly slipped inside. Moving cautiously along the wall, Hadrian felt his way deeper into the cave, presenting the torch to every inlet and cavity in the hope of seeing a sparkling reflection shining back at him. His eyes became used to the dark, but he often stumbled over rock debris strewn over the floor. His cave came to an abrupt halt and he was soon emerging, disappointed at the lack of any indication of evidence of the Universe Bag. After four shallower caves had been examined without excitement, Hadrian arrived at the dip in the wall. He immediately loped towards the nearer group of rocks, still favouring his sore leg. He had to stoop into the first cave he came across and had one painful reminder of the condition of the top of his head when he scraped it on a small, ragged stalactite. This cave, though quite roomy, yielded nothing. The next was equally unexciting but the one following was much deeper. Hadrian and his feeble light probed slowly and deeply right to the very inner reaches of the split in the rock. Again he hit zilch and started retracing his steps towards the mouth of the cave. Half way to the entrance he became aware of the noise of something moving at the mouth of the cave. He couldn't see the opening from where he was and became slightly nervous at the sound. It was a sort of swishing sound followed by a pause. He didn't know why but Hadrian immediately imagined a crocodile heaving its body across the moon's surface while swishing its heavy tail left and right. He edged a little towards the mouth of the cave and stopped again to listen. The noise was coming from immediately outside the opening but still there was nothing to be seen. Hadrian hoped he hadn't stumbled into some monster's cave and it was now returning to its lair. To have any chance against an attacker, Hadrian would have to get out to the opening of the cave where he could see what was going on. He would also have more room to defend himself if necessary. Listening intently and trying to keep his breath quiet, he inched forward, believing that the outside sound was moving on past the cave entrance.

Striding the last few yards, Hadrian placed the torch in his inside pocket and emerged in time to catch a glimpse of Deathbringer dragging Lantar's corpse towards the other group of rocks. He stepped back into the shadows and watched. It was definitely the same Deathbringer which had been fighting Lantar, with the signs of battle very obvious. It had a grip of one neck under its arm and was dragging the rest as best it could; drag, rest, drag, rest.

It gradually disappeared round the far corner of the rock island. Hadrian listened to the pattern of drag and rest for about twenty seconds and then made for the corner where the two had disappeared from sight. He carefully peeked round to see the same scene. The Deathbringer seemed intent on taking Lantar to somewhere specific, dragging the corpse with some purpose directly away from Hadrian.

It occurred to Hadrian that this journey may end in Deathbringer HQ, where he might find the Universe Bag. Dragger and dragged moved out of sight round an outcrop of rock and Hadrian seized the opportunity to advance his position to that point.

He cast a sweeping glance above, behind and beside him but there was no sign of any other creatures. If he was nearing the base of the Deathbringers, he would expect to see or hear evidence of their existence. Still, the only sound that broke the silence was the dragging sound of Lantar's body progressing across the crater floor. Hadrian marvelled at the Deathbringer's strength. Not long ago it was lying as if dead after an incredibly exhausting struggle, yet it was keeping a steady rhythm in its progress to wherever it was going. Drag, rest, drag, rest. Hadrian had to resist the temptation to run out and help just to get them where they were going at an increased speed. Instead, he concentrated on keeping out of sight but fully in touch.

This side of the mountain range was particularly covered in a zigzag of fissures and openings, so Hadrian was able to hug the shadows and progress from spot to spot without breaking cover. He was almost slipping into automatic pilot when Deathbringer stopped. Hadrian froze. The gorilla-creature looked carefully in every direction, bent down and lifted two of the necks in both arms and scuttled backwards towards the rock face and out of sight. The speed of the manoeuvre took Hadrian by surprise and he stood still for a few seconds before thinking of advancing. Had Deathbringer been startled? Hadrian peered all around but could see or hear nothing. He sensed that he may well be very near to the Deathbringer's lair. He took out his catapult and a steel ball in readiness. Part of him didn't want to go on, but the thought of the crystals moved his feet forwards. Still clinging to the rocks and maintaining utter silence, Hadrian edged to the very spot where Deathbringer had changed direction .He looked carefully along the rock face.

His heart fell. There were several openings and slits broad enough to accommodate as many Deathbringers as he could count.

He ran to the nearest one and listened intently. There was no sound at all. There was a short passage linking this cave to the next and pale light ventured in to give him some guidance.

Hadrian had to emerge into the main crater to access the third and then the fourth caves, both of which he investigated briefly. The fifth cave was deeper. It was still cloaked in total silence, so Hadrian chanced getting out the torch and putting his catapult away. The weak beam played on the walls and floor without any surprises. There was nothing for it but to go on. As soon as he set foot into a main passage heading off at an angle towards a deeper mystery, a sixth sense told Hadrian that the sixth cave was the one. He replaced the torch inside his hoodie. He felt the pains in his head and calf for the first time in a while and he could hear his heart thumping. Progressing inwards with great caution, Hadrian began to doubt his instincts. There was not sound nor sight anywhere. He could not see in front of him. He pulled out the torch and held it up above his head. It was removed from his hand. No noise, no ceremony, no threats, just the removal of the disc with complete ease.

Panic flowed through Hadrian and he swivelled round to bolt away as best he could in the pitch dark. He was pushed in the chest so violently he flew backwards and crashed into the cave wall. This was no rock wall. As he hit it he set up a wave of movement along the section of yielding wall and heard a sound like bamboo curtains, wind chimes and loud glockenspiels as his back smacked against it. Before he had any time to make sense of what was happening he was lifted off his feet and pushed through a gap in the 'soft' wall. He flailed out at whatever had lifted him but by the time any of his blows may have struck, he was lying flat on his back in a confused state. He looked up and saw his torch being stuck into a ledge above him, casting its contribution to the light supplied by another ten discs strategically placed to light up the cave.

Deathbringer stared down at him and he gawped at it. It seemed to be sealing up the opening in the cave wall that Hadrian had flown through. Hadrian gasped as he noticed the wall. It was made of scores of Zapro scales, interlocked and overlapping and obviously carefully constructed. Deathbringer was covered in the same rectangular plates. Were the walls constructed of dead Deathbringers and Zapro hides? He turned his head slowly to the left and made out the heaped form of Lantar, dumped unceremoniously against a rock wall. Bits of robots were neatly stored near to Lantar and chunks of what looked like large metal trays were stacked next to them. Deathbringer moved towards Hadrian, who immediately turned his head back into a forward-looking direction. The creature firmly, but not excessively, kicked the sole of Hadrian's foot. Hadrian instinctively wriggled backwards. Another tap in the same place and Hadrian kept moving backwards until he came into contact with a fascinating shape.

Deathbringer, presumably, had stuffed and woven Zapro leather into a comfortable floor cushion. Mesh, with more leather interwoven through it, was wedged into the rock in several places. This served as a soft back to the cushion.

Deathbringer pointed to the cushion and Hadrian scrambled onto it. From here he could see the whole cave. It was incredibly orderly. He was sitting facing the false wall. To its left was Lantar, the robot bits and slabs of metal. Hadrian wondered what creatures were made from the metal trays. The roof was mostly covered in Zapro mesh with a variety of materials interwoven with it, which gave the rock the impression of a ceiling. He leaned back to look above his head and sank into the soft leather comfort behind him. Deathbringer had strung some sort of cable from one side of the ceiling to the other and various lengths of cable-like string and miscellaneous objects dangled from it. Immediately to Hadrian's left were two complete Zapro mesh sacs reinforced with threaded robot spikes and lengths of Zapro necks into huge baskets. The one nearer to his elbow was quite full of heads, bits of mouth blades and teeth, while the other seemed to be full of the clamps, levers, screwdrivers and crimpers taken from robots.

On his right hand was a small container made of small rocks holding a pile of Zapro eyes, a huge heap of haspira piled against the wall and what looked like a makeshift cupboard constructed of slabs which had been soldered together for strength and had a system of hinges on what Hadrian presumed was the door. If it was the door, then the clamp attached to the edge further away from him must have been the handle. These Deathbringers were certainly highly-intelligent thought Hadrian as he watched his captor re-stitching some of the damaged flapping tiles on its leg and arms. Hadrian sat and marvelled at the creature. Deathbringer flashed glances towards him as it was working. Hadrian smiled uncertainly but elicited no response.

He wondered why he hadn't communicated using the scrambler. He wondered what Deathbinger did with all these bits and pieces.

Hadrian scarcely moved while Deathbringer repaired most of its loosened tiles, leaving only the cracked, sliced and almost amputated ones to be done. It ambled towards Hadrian, staring straight at him. Hadrian was convinced those eyes were at least part gorilla. It reached out and prodded him, then prodded the haspira. It was offering him some. Hadrian took a sizeable bunch but instead of putting it into his own mouth he proferred the haspira to Deathbringer. It stared at him for many seconds. Hadrian stared back. The moment was suspended in time as each of them stared and had their thoughts. Eventually, it reached forward and took the food, stuffing it behind overlapping plates where a gorilla's mouth would have been. They were chomped quickly.

It reached into the haspira and offered Hadrian the

handful.

"Thank you," he said filling his mouth and munching. His captor shuffled over to the centre of the cave where a small circle of rocks were formed. It bundled some of the strands hanging from the ceiling cable and placed them in the circle. Stretching up to its full height, it slid two panels to one side revealing a natural chimney in the roof of the cave. Lifting something the size of an egg from a ledge, it proceeded to rub it swiftly against a robot crimper until sparks soon showered on to the cables which combusted immediately. When they were burning well, it reached over and put one main eye on the flames. The eye spluttered into flame and raged into a blaze. The smoke swirled about but did make its way out through the chimney.

As Hadrian watched in amazement, Deathbringer used a particular strand of metal and heated it at one end until white hot. It then ran the heated end over all the cracked plates and discs on its body, sealing them. A strong smell of melting plastic and hot metal confirmed the scene for Hadrian.

That task complete, Deathbringer carefully replaced an almost amputated plate and repeated the process for it and any other. Its last job was to replace a side head plate which had been shaved away to paper thin dimensions by Lantar's mouth blade. It knocked out the tile easily and selected an identical one from its heap. Hadrian noticed that inside its head the Deathbringer had a blanket of pure white strands of circuit wire or something similar. The plate was clapped into position and a swift and expert soldering job completed, just as the fire was giving signs of giving up. Body restored, Deathbringer made its way over to Lantar's body and dragged it away from the wall. Using some of the robot tools, it started the considerable task of dismantling its vanquished enemy. Hadrian decided it was time to talk.

"My name is Hadrian. I come from the planet Earth. Can we communicate using the scrambler?" As if to give further explanation, Hadrian touched himself on his forehead.

Deathbringer stared at Hadrian for what seemed an eternity and then shook its head. Hadrian's breath caught. It had understood. Apparently it could not use the scrambler but it understood.

"Are there more of you?" he asked, only to receive another shake of the head.

"Is Darkbeast one of you?"

This time, Deathbringer slowly stood up and skirted round the glowing fire. Hadrian thought he had angered the beast with the question, but it wasn't heading for him. Rather, it opened the cupboard on his right and withdrew a clear tube of sorts. It handed it to Hadrian. It was the oxygen bubble he had discarded when he met the Dugiri.

"You are Darkbeast! And you are Deathbringer too!" Hadrian wondered why this hadn't occurred to him before. It was friend to those who are peace-loving and enemy of those who choose violence. One creature

– two personalities. Hadrian stared at his oxygen bubble and said, "I'm much happier now that you're Darkbeast, I was a bit scared of Deathbringer."

Darkbeast clapped his hands and gave Hadrian a playful nudge which nearly knocked him off the cushion. Hadrian felt much better. The creature settled down to continue turning Lantar into recyclable scrap. Hadrian watched one head being slit off at the neck, some cuboid inner part removed and slung into an improvised metal/plastic box in the corner where Lantar had been. The eyes were popped out from the inside of the skull and thrown into their box. What was left of the head was tossed on top of the pile of heads in the basket. Darkbeast lifted the next head.

"Can I help you?" asked Hadrian, withdrawing his knife. He opened the blades and held it towards Darkbeast. The creature leaned forward, took the knife and examined it carefully. Looking directly into Hadrian's eyes, it gave a growling wail as if in pain. Gooseflesh flashed up and down Hadrian's back and neck.

CHAPTER 11

What on earth had happened? Hadrian stared as Darkbeast regained its composure. Hadrian was almost certain a tear had fallen from its face but it was too dusky to see properly.

"Wh-what's wrong?" Hadrian's voice was trembling.

Darkbeast stared at him. It seemed to be looking straight through him to some far off memory. It slowly pushed the blades in one by one until only the saw blade was left extended. Placing the knife down next to the entangled limp head, Darkbeast looked up at Hadrian then patted the ground beside the knife. Hadrian took this as an invitation to join in the dismantling and stood up and walked round behind Darkbeast to his appointed space. As he squatted down to work, still a little nervously, a beautiful array of winking crystals sent the fire's reflected light into his eyes from within the cupboard. Darkbeast had left the door open when he had extricated the oxygen mask. The Universe Bag sat proudly among an assembly of odd 'trophies' and curios. His heart leaped but after what had just happened, he did not mention the Bag just yet. He picked up his knife and slowly sawed away at the mesh which trapped the head he was seeking. Both of them sat in silence, Hadrian freeing the head and Darkbeast finishing with the other and starting to dismantle the plates and tile shapes which made up the neck. They seemed to be held together by leathery thongs and Darkbeast expertly cut one end and threaded the thong through a maze of interconnecting holes and short tubes until he could get no further with it. He would trim it off to hang at the ceiling later. Returning to the top, he would painstakingly repeat this procedure for another thong and so on until the plate or plates fell free. As the sections fell away and the neck was stripped down, a confusion of wires, clips and junction circles were seen inside. The junction circles were like little fat spiders with about forty legs each, every one linking with other wires and boxes until Darkbeast ripped them free.

Hadrian was working as hard as he could but was making slow progress compared to Darkbeast. The light in the cave wasn't much now that the fire was almost out, although it didn't seem to matter to Darkbeast who was well down the central neck when Hadrian finally freed the last bit of buried mesh from the head. He triumphantly sawed off the head and handed it to Darkbeast. It clapped and took it, removing the same cuboid shape. Hadrian offered his hand and it was placed in it. It was wet and metallic. Although it was slippery to hold, he managed to toss it into the box he had seen the other one thrown into. In the meantime, two eyes had been tossed into the eye bank and the third, very damaged one was placed on the fire. It immediately spluttered to life giving much improved light and a little heat. Darkbeast indicated the mesh, empty of leathery fronds.

"Shall I remove this next?"

Darkbeast nodded once, then turned to its own task. Whether Hadrian was getting better at it or whether the collisions of battle had served to weaken grips, this mesh was coming off much more easily than that which had wrapped round the head. Some of Darkbeast's net was still wrapped round the lower neck Hadrian had been working on and that made his job awkward. Despite this, he had time to watch Darkbeast do the strangest thing. From within the neck, he pulled out a red slab, roughly circular in shape and the size of Hadrian's hand. Spearing it with robot arm, he set it aside and retrieved another, very similar disc and subjected it to the same treatment. Having them both skewered, he placed them into the fire, with the ends resting on the rocks. Hadrian kept half an eye on them and half on his work as they spat and sizzled and gave off an aroma of smoked bacon mixed with rubber. When both had turned pure white, Darkbeast removed them and placed them on a tile each. Using a blade removed from a robot hand, it sliced through one of them, pierced it through with the point of his blade and raised it under the overlapping tiles to where its mouth obviously was. It made chewing sounds for ages before lifting the other part of the disc and repeating the procedure. It pushed the other plate to Hadrian.

He wasn't sure, but trimmed off about one sixth of the white shape and put it reluctantly in his mouth. He remembered his father telling him once that fox meat was inedible. This had to be fox meat. He chewed and chewed and chewed to avoid swallowing. There was no way he could force this over. It was like eating the smell of silage. Hadrian spat it out into the fire when he could stand it no longer.

"I'm sorry, Darkbeast, that is revolting!" he exclaimed.

Darkbeast clapped its hands and retrieved the remainder of Hadrian's and finished it.

Hadrian removed Lantar's complete sac just as Darkbeast had returned from placing all his recycled bits in their appropriate places. On its way it had closed over the cupboard door casually and so the bag was out of sight again. Darkbeast demonstrated where and how to cut the thongs as he threw more coiled heat on the fire. Hadrian managed and started the complex of task of threading, when the heat in the cave and the excitement of the day overtook him and he dozed off – in short fits initially and then into a deep and restful slumber. Darkbeast carried him gently over to the cushion and laid him down. It sat on the floor just watching him sleep. Had Hadrian opened his eyes then, he would have seen two huge tears rolling down interlocking cheek plates, but Hadrian was totally out, beyond even the land of dreams.

He awoke to find that Darkbeast had completed the dismantling of Lantar and was arranging more of the mesh to hold a variety of complete and cracked tiles over the ceiling and down walls, presumably for insulation. The discs of torchlight had all been moved to Hadrian's end of the cave and two strange contraptions were standing near him. They were like tall floor lamps without light bulbs, constructed from robot and neck innards, but for what purpose he could not tell. His knife had been placed closed beside him and he put it away. He wondered why he didn't feel the need to go to the toilet. He sat up and wished Darkbeast a good morning. It clapped and nodded and continued to slip the plates behind the supporting mesh. Hadrian went over and lifted a tile for his host. So they worked until the area covered by the mesh was saturated with whole and fragmented plates. Darkbeast indicated to Hadrian to sit on the cushion and offered him haspira. Hadrian declined the haspira and sat up on the cushion. He wondered what was coming.

Darkbeast shuffled over to the left wall as Hadrian viewed it and picked up a large flat slab of silver metal. As it lifted it over towards Hadrian, he noticed that four inverted Zapro heads had been soldered onto the corners as short legs. Darkbeast put the table down in front of

Hadrian. It then lifted the large floor lamp contraption to his left and rammed it one third way into a crevice at its own head height. Hadrian was equally puzzled when it repeated the action with the one on the other side. It gave a clap and wandered into the far recesses of the left-hand side of its home. It dragged out a large lidded box of leather, mesh and interwoven cable construction.

Darkbeast stared at Hadrian from just beyond the extinguished fire. It would be more accurate to say it looked through him. Hadrian sensed that it was making its mind up about something. He was desperate to try to get the crystals but having got so near to them, he didn't want to mess it all up. What could be in the box? It flipped the lid open but then in what seemed to be a change of mind it went back into a bag in the corner and emerged with two of the little cuboid shapes it had removed from Zapro heads. It pointed to Hadrian's pocket.

"My knife? Do you want my knife?" A single nod let Hadrian know he was right first time and he handed it up to this strange creature. Choosing a thin blade, Darkbeast somehow connected the cuboid to the cables of the protruding lamp structure. Having inspected its work, it twisted two wires round a metallic tube and the entire length of cabled robot bit winked rapidly and repeatedly like a fluorescent tube being switched on, then flooded the area with much brighter light. Hadrian's eyes smarted and he shut them.

He could hear Darkbeast applaud then fix up the

other lamp in the same way. The whole cave was lit by a light that was no brighter than his main bedroom light at home, but it seemed so much brighter here in Darkbeast's home. With the table well lit, the creature went to the cupboard and opened the door wide. The crystals sparkled like fireworks. Hadrian took the bull by the horns.

"The Universe Bag! That's why I'm here on the moon: to recover that bag for Grior. Do you remember Grior with the Dugiri?" Darkbeast stared at Hadrian, so he went on, "He's from Jupiter, smaller than me, has a ball as his feet and three arms. His head's a funny shape and he's got one eye which can move all around!"

Darkbeast held up the crystals till they dazzled resplendently in the stronger light. They reflected on its face and round the walls. It seemed to be thinking. Hadrian wondered if he dared ask for it but before he could decide, Darkbeast put the bag back in its place and brought out what had all the appearance of a hard-cover notebook. It was almost loose from its stitching and was damaged by fire by the looks of it but it resembled any book you might see on earth. It was laid gently down in front of Hadrian and turned round to face him correct way up. The cover was very faded with something written on it.

"Where did you get this?"

Darkbeast pointed to itself. It then lifted something from the cupboard and mimed it spiralling down and down until it smacked on the table. Hadrian gave a little jump. When Darkbeast slid his hand off the small tray of metal, there was the flag of the United States of America emblazoned on it.

"A space ship! A crashed space ship" shouted Hadrian excitedly, "You got this from a crashed space ship?"

Darkbeast nodded. "And the book, from the same ship?" Again it nodded. Hadrian felt a strong thrill course through his veins as he stared at the book. Darkbeast clapped and when it had Hadrian's attention it pointed to the table top, to a piece of Perspex in the ceiling mesh, to some sheets of metal in the door and wall coverings leaning stacked against the wall.

"You got all of those things from a crashed space ship?"

It pointed to itself.

"Is there any of it left where it crashed? Was there anyone on board?" It nodded to each of these and pointed to the book. Hadrian looked with great care at the writing on it. It wasn't much. It seemed to be two short words. The first letter could have been a capital 'A' but then he saw another bit to it. It was an 'N'. Yes, an 'N'.... or an 'M'. Nj? Aj? Mj? My? That was it! 'My'

My what? Another very short word as before. Like an 'a' or an 'o' in the middle and a j or y at the end again. Possibly a three letter word. Could be a capital 'L' at the start: My lay, my laj, my loj my loy- My log!

"MY LOG!" shouted Hadrian. He looked up at

Darkbeast which had retreated to the open-lidded box again. What happened next was astonishing. Darkbeast worked at one paw and then the other until the covering of tiles fell off, landing on the floor with a tinkling sound.

Two black human hands wrenched the head off the shoulders to reveal a very tall, very black human being's head. The head had thick, silvery white hair which tumbled down way past the shoulders and midway down the back.

"Y-you're a man," squeaked Hadrian feebly, wondering if this world could possibly hold any more surprises for him. The black human unclipped, untied and undid hidden fastenings in his body armour and carefully lowered it to the floor. His shoulders were immense and his arm muscles rippled powerfully as he removed his leggings, stepped out of his boots and placed them with the others. Hadrian was staring at a black, very powerfully built human male. The male turned round so he had his back to Hadrian. He was totally naked yet Hadrian felt no awkwardness or embarrassment when surveying his every move. He watched him step into a shabby silver/white kind of boiler suit and pull it up over his shoulders. He turned slowly to face Hadrian. The suit had a United States of America flag as a flash on its left shoulder, the letters 'N.A.S.A. 1964' on a wave-shaped chest-lapel bearing tiny wings at either corner. On the flap of his breast pocket was stitched the name 'Chuck Giemza'.

Hadrian tried to take in all that he was seeing and thinking and he was seeing and thinking an awful lot. The human moved easily nearer to him.

"You are an astronaut." This was a statement by Hadrian but the astronaut nodded in agreement anyway. "Are you Chuck?" He nodded in reply. "How do you pronounce your surname? Is it Geemza?" this received an abrupt shake of the white flowing locks. "Gee-emza?"

Chuck's pronounced nod verified his identity and Hadrian stared on, trying to piece together the story that was unfolding before him.

"You landed on the moon on a crashed space ship, in 1964?"

Chuck nodded.

"But according to the history books a Russian cosmonaut called 'Yuri Gagarin' was the first man into space in 1966. How come we never heard of your mission?"

Giemza put a finger up to his lips in a shushing motion.

"Top secret? But why? Was it for political reasons?"

Chuck reached his forefinger and thumb into his breast pocket and pulled out a torn piece of card. He handed it to Hadrian. Despite it being torn it bore the wording 'Apollo Mission SH.'

The next passage of time was spent with Hadrian having a few wrong guesses and then hit a correct one in trying to build the story from the astronaut's mimes and facial expressions.

He had finally gleaned that the USA was desperately trying to win the space race and land a man on the moon before the Russians. The entire mission was highest category secret. Hadrian let a long low whistle escape from his cheeks. "Why can't you speak, Chuck?" he asked and watched as Giemza walked up to him, dropped to his knees in front of him and opened his mouth wide. Teeth yes, tongue no. "Oh, jeez, I'm so sorry"

Chuck clapped and shrugged. Hadrian was full of questions.

"Why do you wear that body armour, Chuck?"

The astronaut pointed to the basket of Zapro heads by way of explanation.

"But they're all destroyed now, aren't they?"

Chuck shook his head and stuck two fingers in the air towards the entrance.

"Two more? Were they not in the crater in the battle?"

Chuck put his hand above his eyes in a pose of looking into the distance. After a few attempts at deciphering the mime, Hadrian guessed correctly that Chuck was portraying scouts who were out on duty at the time of the attack. An idea occurred to Hadrian.

"Why not come back with me, Chuck? We can both use the travel crystals to return to Earth. You may end up in my bedroom but they may return you to your own home or to NASA!" Chuck reached in and brought out the Universe Bag from his cupboard. He held it in both hands, slowly jostling the contents about while staring at them.

"The capsules transport you. The Earth crystal is missing because Grior used part of it. I have it in my pocket. One bite and you can return as a hero! Just think of the effect you'd have returning after all these years!" Hadrian looked imploringly at Chuck Giemza as the astronaut seemed to ponder what he had just heard. He still passed the bag from hand to hand, letting the contents tumble over each other within the container. After some time, he laid the crystals back on the cupboard shelf and went back to the box in the far recesses of the cave. He rummaged in the box for a few moments and then stood up holding a dilapidated folder of sorts. 'What is he bringing now,' thought Hadrian as his gaze fell onto the log book lying in front of him.

*

CHAPTER 12

Chuck squatted across the makeshift table from Hadrian. He held the folder to his chest with his arms across it like the cross on a Scottish flag. Hadrian could sense a feeling of emotional energy welling up in the cave. Chuck just stared at him as if trying to decide what to do. Hadrian carefully opened the log book at a page badly singed and torn. He made out the words; "Moon in view. Beautiful. Typical Jake singing 'Fly me to the Moon'! All going wel..." but the rest was lost in the damage to the page.

"Jake? Was there another astronaut called Jake?"

Chuck nodded.

"Did he survive the crash too?"

The sad expression on Chuck's face was all Hadrian needed in order to know the answer to his question. "So the USA tried to land two astronauts on the moon, to beat Russia?" Hadrian asked, but Chuck wagged his finger 'no' and then stuck three fingers upwards.

"Three!?" Hadrian looked at the next page in the log, hoping to find the third spaceman's name. The page only displayed the words; 'Thinking of home. With any luck we...' As he slowly picked his way through the fire-damaged bits of paper there was little that was legible on any of the pages. There were odd words and scraps of sketches or part of a phrase, mostly concerned with instrument data and flight information. As he pored meticulously over each part page for any additional information, Chuck stood up and placed his folder on top of the cupboard. He stooped into a deep shelf in the cave wall and emerged with a handful of a substance which looked like petroleum jelly. He scooped haspira into it and proceeded to mix them thoroughly, adding pinches of sand from the cold fire until he had a grey paste. Leaning over Hadrian, he gently spread the mixture over the cut and bump on the top of his head. Hadrian stopped turning pages and closed his eyes in a heavenly feeling of his entire head being soothed and refreshed. Chuck massaged him gently for a few minutes then left the wound covered by the paste.

He applied some to his own bruises and scrapes. Hadrian pulled up the damaged leg of his jeans to show Chuck his very bruised calf. Astronaut Giemza carefully spread the last of the mixture over the inflamed calf and massaged it with a firm, circular motion. Hadrian gritted his teeth and tried not to show it, but this cure was more painful than the injury! Gradually, the aches subsided and eventually left his calf completely. Chuck rubbed the last of the paste away and Hadrian's calf was restored to full health. The throbbing in his head had diminished to no more than an itch. Chuck shuffled over to the corner and emerged with a strip of teeth which had had their sharp points rounded. As if to explain to Hadrian, the astronaut combed his long hair with his home-made comb. His white hair shone in stark contrast to his dark skin. He gently combed the dried blood and paste out of Hadrian's hair. Out along with the paste and dirt and blood went the pain and aches in Hadrian's head. By the time Chuck had cleaned the last remnants of dried blood, all pain had gone altogether.

"That's cool, Chuck! I wish we had that kind of paste on Earth!"

Chuck smiled for the first time and replaced the comb in its corner. Hadrian turned his attention to the log again, continuing to flip over pages with part words and incomplete phrases visible on undamaged areas. After many fruitless pages he turned to one which had the following entry: 'Thanx for a page in yer cookery book Chuck. Popeye'

On the facing page was, 'Popeye's Moon Poem'

'Me be on the moon soon

Soon be on the moon

No monsoon on cool moon

Is boon, moon not monsooned.'

Hadrian read out the poem and smiled. "Was 'Popeye' the other astronaut?"

A slight nod of the head confirmed this. "I take it he

was killed too?" The question didn't really need an answer and didn't get one as Chuck seemed to have drifted miles away in distracted thoughts.

"If his poetry is an example of his humour, he and my dad would have got on well," continued Hadrian as he flicked over a few more pages. On the very last page that had anything written on it, the part message had survived; ' ..orrow we land. God bless us and protect us one and a..' Hadrian closed over the log book carefully and handed it up to Chuck. He replaced it in the cupboard and then looked at the folder on top of the cabinet, glancing between it and Hadrian several times as if still having difficulty in coming to a decision. His mind made up, he lifted the folder and placed it on the table. He squatted cross-legged, nestling the base of the folder on the top of his thighs and the top of it on the edge of the table. He reached inside and after a little shuffling brought out a faded colour photograph. He turned it round to face Hadrian, flipped it over face-side down and pushed it across the table. Hadrian read the information on the back. 'Chuck Giemza, NASA training, 1964' He turned the photograph over and despite the many cracks and folds, there was the snapshot of a very proud astronaut in full gear, holding his helmet at his waist and smiling radiantly with pride at the camera. The hair was short and jet black but the face was still easily recognisable as Chuck.

"This must have been taken shortly before your mission, Chuck." The back of another photo appeared near Hadrian, this time with the description; ' Jake, Chuck and Popeye on Apollo program training, May 1964' Hadrian found that his hand was slightly shaky as he looked at the scene on the front. The men were all in dungaree sets, Chuck in the middle being slightly taller than the other two. All three were sporting huge grins. Chuck had one arm round Jake's shoulder and the other resting on Popeye's with a finger pointing in mock menace in his friend's ear, thumb cocked as if it was a pistol. Popeye had short red curly hair and was stockier than Chuck. He had both his arms stuck out towards the camera with each giving a 'thumbs up' sign. He also had his eyes crossed.

Jake was balding and athletically built. He had one arm wrapped round Chuck's shoulder and the other holding a small flag of the USA aloft. He was winking at the camera.

Hadrian took some time to absorb the scene. He had never met Popeye nor Jake yet could feel himself getting emotional just looking at these three guys, full of life and fun, two of whom were now dead. The other was living in exile, presumed dead and totally uncelebrated because of the secret nature of his mission. He wondered how the US government had explained away the loss of three astronauts. Probably reported as killed in training; some ghastly fire possibly to avoid the need for identifiable bodies. Wait till he got back to Earth. He could take Chuck home! What a stir that would cause. He glanced up at his friend. "I'm really sorry about your friends, Chuck, I wish there was something I could do."

Chuck shrugged his shoulders, then delved back into the folder. This time he brought out a very dog-eared page from a newspaper. It was turning brown and had darker lines running along the folds. At the top was displayed, 'The New York Times page 6 31st August 1962'

Halfway down the page was a large photograph of a family of husband, wife and son. The article was headed; 'Wisconsin Astronaut Top of the Class.' Hadrian read on. 'Charles (Chuck) Giemza from Eau Claire, Wisconsin, has passed out top of Astronaut Advanced Training School last Wednesday. Chuck gained an overall assessment of 96%, the highest score ever achieved in the history of the course. A spokesman for The Kennedy Centre said, "Chuck is an extra special guy. He is respected by all his buddies in the program and shows real impressive understanding of all aspects of space travel. We'll sure miss him. Chuck was presented with a special medal and scroll by Colonel Luke (Sky) Walker of NASA. Pictured at the ceremony is Chuck with his wife Beverley and their six-year-old son Myles.'

Even though the newspaper was so old, Hadrian would have been able to recognise Chuck without the caption. Beverley Giemza was strikingly beautiful. She was black, tall and slim with long curls cascading down to her shoulders. Her smile was as broad as Chuck's.

His little son Myles was looking proudly forward, with his Afro style hair sitting atop a cute face and a delighted grin. He was holding up Chuck's medal towards the photographer. Hadrian felt a lump in his throat and realised how much he missed his own parents at that particular moment.

"Does your family think you're dead?"

Chuck shrugged and nodded and retrieved the cutting, folding it meticulously before sliding it into the folder.

"Chuck, I'm sure we could use Grior's crystals for both of us to return safely to Earth. You would be able to see your family again. Chuck stared off into the distance with fresh tears welling up in his eyes. Hadrian wished he could do something to help, but was all out of ideas.

Chuck looked into the folder and brought out yet another photograph. He slid it across face down again. Hadrian read the back and wasn't sure he wanted to turn it over. Scrawled on the bag was 'Myles' 8th birthday'. After a short pause he did turn it over, to be faced with a huge smile, big brown eyes and Afro curls. Myles was wearing a new baseball cap and pitcher's glove. A baseball nestled in the glove. In his other hand he was holding up a basketball and hanging from his trouser belt was a Swiss army knife, identical to Hadrian's. So that was why Chuck had reacted so animatedly on seeing his knife. It was all too much for Hadrian. Perhaps it was because he was suddenly acutely aware of family or the effect of this cute little kid looking so happily out at him, but Hadrian burst into tears. He launched himself forward into Chuck's muscular arms and the two of them hugged and wept unashamedly.

When he was able to regain some of his composure, he repeated his earlier suggestion to Chuck that they could both make use of the Earth crystal and travel pods to return to their home. He explained to Chuck how the crystals worked and summarised Grior's story and his own mission. He finished by asking, "Will you come back with me?"

Chuck stared at Myles' photo and shook his head to mean 'no'. He placed his thumb at Myles' feet and his forefinger on his head. Keeping the thumb still, he slid his finger further up the snap to indicate that his son would have grown considerably by now. He touched his wrist where a watch would have been and made little circular movements to signify time passing. Hadrian understood both sets of signals and nodded his head in sad sympathy. He pulled his knife from his pocket and held it out to Chuck, pointing to Myles's knife.

"This is a present for you, Chuck, to remind you of Myles. It might come in useful, too."

Chuck accepted it and laid it in the palm of his hand, stroking it with the other. After a while he gathered all his folder contents together and put it back in its storage box. He took the knife to his cupboard and placed it amongst his prized possessions.

He returned to Hadrian holding the dazzling bag of

multi-coloured crystals, glittering fiercely in the strong light of the new lamps.

He offered the bag to Hadrian who clutched it with emotional relief coursing through him. The Universe bag! He had it! He had achieved his mission after all. What an absolutely incredible adventure it had been. It was the journey of space dreams; the Dugiri, Jurgat and Pintar especially; Darkbeast and Deathbringer being the same beast and both of them being Chuck. Zapro and Lantar; haspira; that incredible air swimming cave; the moon's landscape; the battles; the story of the secret moon launch that went wrong and this brilliant bag of crystals.

Hadrian looked at Chuck. "I should return to Earth. Grior will be anxious – and probably my parents too by now. Are you sure you won't come with me?"

Chuck reached out and touched the bag. He indicated with nodding head and slight pressure of his hand on Hadrian's that Hadrian should put the bag in a pocket. Somewhat puzzled, Hadrian allowed his hand to be pushed towards his hoodie pocket and carefully stuffed the bag well in.

Chuck made a thumbs-up sign, squatted back down and pointed to Hadrian and himself and then the cave door. He then made his hands into fists and started waving them about in all directions making a noise in the back of his nose to imitate speed. When he got no response from Hadrian he repeated his actions, occasionally bringing one fist down with a smack into his other palm. He then pretended to eat from his open palm.

"The Dugiri! You're miming the movement of the Dugiri and them making haspira"

Chuck nodded and mimed further a Dugiri fist, then he pointed to Hadrian and finally he made a 'waving goodbye' motion. The hand waving goodbye finished moving by pointing to the pocket containing the Universe Bag. Hadrian understood right away.

"You want me to go and say goodbye to the Dugiri and then bite the crystal, don't you? Will you come with me?"

Chuck's vigorous nodding made Hadrian realise that the astronaut had always intended to accompany him. He repeated his pointing at Hadrian, himself and the cave door as he nodded.

"That's a great idea, Chuck. I owe the Dugiri a huge thanks and would like to see if Pintar survived the battle or not." Chuck sprang to life and beckoned Hadrian over to his stash of Zapro body parts. He repeated a mime indicating that at least two Zapro scouts could still be active and proceeded to make Hadrian a basic coat of armour. First he found a neck and slipped it on like a sleeve to one arm. Scratching a mark on a plate at the wrist, he removed the sleeve, snipped it to size and put it back. The armour was remarkably light to wear. A section was cut like a short cloak and set against Hadrian's back. While he tried to hold bits in position, Chuck threaded Hadrian's cloak and sleeves together so they fitted remarkably snugly as one piece. He then turned his attention to the legs. Two wider necks were fitted using the same method as for the arms and then a wide section originally cut from just above the leathery sac was placed on Hadrian's torso. With snipping and trimming at the armpits and waist, the breastplate was soon a comfortable fit. Chuck wove it to the cloak section then linked each leg to it.

Having gone to such care to create the one-piece suit of armour, he then cut down the centre of the front and made hidden loops so that Hadrian would be able to open the suit to take it off and fasten it behind overlapping tiles for security. This part of work took the longest by far. As Chuck fastened him up for the final fitting, Hadrian made sure his catapult and ammo were in left-sided pockets he could slip his right hand into. Once totally suited up, he practised slipping a loop or two open to access map and weapon and the closing again using a single hand. Chuck's loops and toggles were so expert that Hadrian was soon opening and closing like a cowboy going for his gun in a shoot-out. The Bag was pocketed low on his right, the most protected part of the body armour. Hadrian could not believe how light it was. He tried some moves and turns as Chuck expertly donned his suit. The two of them stood looking like two things from a robot world but feeling secure in their protective covers.

Chuck extinguished the bright lights and ate a large quantity of haspira. Hadrian still had a little in his pocket, but also ate his fill from the stock in the cave. He cast his eyes once more round the dimly lit cave that was Chuck's home, then ducked into the pitch dark tunnel as Chuck opened, then closed the hanging tile wall which formed his front door. Chuck led Hadrian carefully along the tunnels until they emerged into the dull light of the crater. They started to cross the crater, Hadrian getting used to the slight restriction on his stride because of his armour. As they neared the boundary, he noticed his home-made sword cum lance he had made, resting where he had left it. Hadrian picked it up. It was nothing compared to Chuck's sword but it might help if they met the Zapro scouts. They scaled the perimeter and headed north-west.

*

CHAPTER 13

They covered the ground at an easy pace, each lost in his own thoughts, but keeping a wary eye for any signs of Zapro. Hadrian broke the silence. "Just give me the thumbs down if I'm out of order, Chuck, but did your tongue get damaged when your space ship crashed?"

Chuck nodded. The two continued in silence until Chuck came to a halt. He prodded at Hadrian's breast pocket. Hadrian pulled out his poster. Chuck clapped and made a series of prods from the bottom to the top of the paper.

"Make a map?" asked Hadrian, to which his ally nodded. Chuck then mimed a battle then indicated he and Hadrian flying away in opposite directions.

"I understand! In case we are separated in battle, I'll be able to find the Dugiri."

The next few minutes were spent in running his forefinger over the sheet until he felt the sharp jabs identifying target areas and landmarks. The first port of call was the crater Backlund, due north from their present position. After that the mountain of Montes Pyranaeus was indicated north west of the crater. Hadrian replaced the poster having had enough jabs for the moment and set off due north. The journey was unremarkable and they gathered speed as they glided easily across the flat surface. Backlund soon loomed and Chuck slowed to walking speed as they approached it. He signalled Hadrian to come to him and they scrambled up the loose stones and over the edge. Chuck led Hadrian round the side of a crescent-shaped rock formation and pointed to the hollow area which came into view as they turned the corner. Chuck had obviously been here a few times as a lot of work had been done. There, side by side, lay two neat and well-tended graves. The one on the left was covered in silvery blue Zapro plates and the other with ones which were more bluish black. A short pole with an astronaut's helmet on it was at the head of the silver grave. The visor had writing scratched on it; 'Here lie the mortal remains of Jake Early died 1964 RIP. The blue grave had no helmet but had two American flags stuck in the ground at the head. A chunk of matt silver space ship lay wedged between the flags with the words 'Popeye Kennedy rests here. Died 1964. His last wish was that he could wish that the wish wasn't his last one. RIP.'

Hadrian stood in the solemn silence remembering the photograph of the three fun-loving friends and sensing the sadness which still dominated Chuck after all these years. He remembered Popeye's silly poem about the moon and could see he took his wacky humour with him right to the end. Chuck knelt and prayed silently. Hadrian knelt too and thought hard to get inside Chuck's head, as Astronaut Giemza remembered his team and prayed for both of them. When they had finished paying their respects, Chuck turned and headed for Pyranaeus. Hadrian followed right away.

This leg of their journey passed without incident and, as they approached the mountain, Hadrian took out his poster to map the remainder of the journey. The next session seemed to be north east to a wrinkle ridge named Dorsum Guettard, then a sharp switch north east to Appolonius Crater. After that it was time to aim for 10degrees N and 20W, where they should find Copernicus Crater and the Dugiri. He put the map away and set off towards Chuck who had stopped to wait for him just at the point he would disappear round the mountain and out of sight. As he came to a stop, Chuck pointed up the mountain slope towards a tangled mess of metal and loosened debris

"Apollo SH. Your space ship." It wasn't a question. The two trudged up the slope. Chuck hung back. No doubt he had visited here often to scavenge bits and pieces of the spacecraft for his cave. Hadrian surveyed the twisted metal skeleton of the ship. It was partly embedded in the mountainside and the years had dulled the colours of the few sections still attached to the frame.

There were a few stencil markings, but nothing to indicate that it was an American space probe or moon shot. It was strange to think that three buddies had set off into space, full of hope of making their footprint in history, only to end up with two dead and one surviving on the moon. To add to that, the mission had been so secret that their courage had never been made known to the public.

"I know your names now. Just wait till I get back to Earth. I'll tell everyone who'll listen – and those who won't – until the USA admits its deceit and you are given your rightful places in space history."

Chuck clapped his hands, patted Hadrian on the back and gave him a brief hug. All in all this was an awkward, 'clattery' thing to do with the two coats of armour being worn, but nevertheless the emotion was mutually conveyed. After an appropriate time, they headed off towards the wrinkle ridge of Dorsum Guettard. This feature was exactly 20 degrees directly south of Copernicus and 10 degrees south of the crater Apollonius.

It wouldn't be long now before he was saying goodbye to the Dugiri and heading home. Their speed had imperceptibly increased and they were fairly covering the terrain with huge hops, steps and jumps. Wrinkle Ridge was straight ahead and looked totally uninteresting, a long grey blob of ejected lava stuck like a giant blob of chewing gum on the moon's surface. Standing atop it, Hadrian and Chuck stopped only long enough to catch their breath and take a little more haspira each.

"What was that stuff you cooked and offered me in the cave, Chuck?"

Chuck made the 'Z for Zorro' sign in the air. The film Zorro was before Hadrian's time and he had never seen any remake, but to him the Z meant Zapro. Chuck followed making the sign by putting his hand over his heart. He then repeated 'Z' and hand on heart.

"Zapro heart? Yeuch!" spat out Hadrian as Chuck clapped repeatedly in obvious pleasure.

"But you had three or four from the one beast. How many hearts do they have?"

Chuck indicated his neck and then stuck up four fingers.

"Each neck has four hearts? So Lantar had twelve?" Hadrian found it hard to believe but Chuck nodded again and rubbed his tummy the way that's normally done to mean 'delicious'.

"Oh, yucks! I can't believe I actually put that stuff in my mouth."

Chuck flexed his arms as if showing off his muscles, but Hadrian decided that if he was telling him that eating it made you strong, then he would prefer to stay as a weakling. Mind you, he thought, if Chuck crashed on the moon in 1964 he must be somewhere around 70 – 80 years old. He had the physique of a fit man half that age, so maybe eating slabs of slurry was good for you. Why was it that things that everyone said were good for you always tasted horrible? Cod liver oil – or "cod liver 'orrible", as Hadrian called it, for example. Hadrian gave an involuntary shiver and started towards Apollonius Crater. While this crater was well to the east, it was only 5 degrees south of Copernicus over easy terrain. Hadrian felt an excitement rising inside him as his adventure came ever closer to completion. The ridged perimeter of the crater came into view right on line. Hadrian drew up alongside Chuck and let his gaze fall on the jagged silhouette of the rim of the crater's edge.

He thought of Grior and had a secret smile. Not long now. Hadrian felt a slight tug on his arm. He turned to look at Chuck, who nodded at the crater and pointed. Drifting up the side, apparently travelling in the same direction as Chuck and Hadrian, were two Zapro warriors. Hadrian automatically slowed and fished out his catapult and four ball bearings and then balanced his spear in his left hand. Blast it! Trust them to spoil things, he thought as he shadowed Chuck the last few metres towards the crater.

If the Zapro were also travelling north on their scouting duties, the chances were that they hadn't yet noticed them. They would soon know. They took short hops up to the top of the crater's edge and cautiously peeked over into the area below. Suspended twenty metres away, sacs wafting to and fro to maintain the hover position, waited the two Zapro, looking straight up at the two of them. Chuck stood up slowly to his full height and started gently swinging his sword side to side like a pendulum.

Hadrian stood on a rock a little higher than Chuck to appear more of a similar height. He wedged his spear point down in a crack in the rock by his right side and loaded his catapult. No-one spoke. Hadrian noticed that the taller of the two Zapro had a third neck forming. It was only about the length of a ruler, but was definitely evident. Chuck looked all around to ensure they hadn't been lured into an ambush. Only the two scouts hung below. Heads snapping back and shut menacingly at the two travellers. As if by some signal, the Zapro rose together, slowly and in unison until they were at chest height to Chuck, suspended some twenty or so metres away.

Hadrian needed no formal invitation. The two-necked creature offered a better target for its eyes, as the W one had its heads slightly reclined. A mouth shot would be good for it. He placed one ball into the sling, fully extended it and released the lightning fast ball into one mouth of W. He had already reloaded and was aiming straight at one of the V's main eyes when the sound of splintering teeth rent the air. As the second ball was released, the V warrior turned the very head Hadrian had aimed for towards the sound of the shattering material. As a result, the ball only scored a hit on the lower area of a peripheral eye, causing vanilla-coloured fluid to spurt out and dribble in a sticky vomit down the neck. The third ball was loaded as the Zapro lifted their sacs behind them into torpedo position to attack. It smacked a side head on W, cracking loudly. A small hole appeared. He fired off his fourth ball at point blank range as the Zapro torpedoed in. He had no idea where it hit as he ducked, grabbed his spear out of the ground and slashed the nearer V neck to him. He immediately rolled down the crater facing and ducked under a ledge as a neck smacked into his shoulder. It knocked him totally off balance, but luckily it thumped him deeper in against the wall and further under the rock canopy.

He fumbled more ammunition out as the V found a way under the shelf to reach him. Again the catapult was fired with full venom at no distance. It split the blade in the monster's mouth and caused it to jerk its head back momentarily. In that moment Hadrian's spear slashed widely back and forth across head, mouth and eyes, trying desperately to render one of the warrior's heads useless. He stabbed his spear into the same mouth and broke several pieces of teeth. The other teeth managed to grip a shoulder tile and gouge a deep slice off its full length. It didn't snap off because the split blade in its mouth had been knocked to a slight angle and could not exert sufficient purchase to bite off Hadrian's shoulder and neck. However, the other head could.

Chuck had just time to notice Hadrian tumbling down the crater wall when he had to turn his full attention to W. Leaping away from Hadrian, he swung an almighty blow at the nearer head and smacked it just below the mouth blade. While a major crack appeared the mouth blade seemed to be intact. Chuck, unlike Hadrian, had head, foot and hand armour on, too. This was just as well, as he suddenly felt the grip of a partially-toothed head on the top of his, trying to crunch it into brittle. It would probably have succeeded had Hadrian not taken out several of the central teeth with his opening shot. Chuck threw himself against the rock face and gripping his sword like grim death, he swung and kicked and bounced all the way down the jagged rocks. The Zapro was clinging on to his head but was getting buffeted all the way down the wall until they landed with a smack on the crater floor. There was a flint-sharp rock protruding from the floor. The head holding Chuck sliced its hinge muscle right through on the rock and severed itself from its neck. The headless neck beat on Chuck with ferocious strength. He was still trying to come to full consciousness after his tumble when the remaining head clamped onto his thigh. Chuck staggered into an upright position only to have his sword smacked out of his hand and out of reach by the snaking neck.

Had the situation not been so deadly, it would have been comic. Chuck was standing with one head clamped into his armour at thigh level, a headless neck was thrashing him with loud, damaging wallops and that neck's head was severed and still gripped onto the top of Chuck's head like a preposterous hat.

Hadrian was totally taken by surprise by the crunching sound of his other shoulder being clamped by the other head. He had been paying too much attention to the other one. He had no time to wallow in regrets as the two heads worked together to yank him unceremoniously out from under the ledge at speed . He cracked his head on the way out and could feel blood running down his hair and ear as he was released by the damaged head while the other held him by the bleeding neck and shoulder armour. It raised him up a few metres from the crater bed, ready to smash him down to instant death. Hadrian knew he was going to lose consciousness. Just before he did he saw Chuck down below with a head attached to his own, another to his leg and a neck beating him down onto one knee. His sword glinted some five metres from him on the crater floor. He passed out.

Chuck struggled desperately, but as he was pushed over, he noticed Hadrian dangling from the V's mouth. As his back hit the floor the swarm of Dugiri struck. He felt the lightning rat-a-tat of his flying friends as they bombed the clamped head until it released its grip and tried to defend itself. It didn't stand a chance. The group of Dugiri formed a circle of about forty, in the air above Chuck. They dive bombed in quick-fire succession, impacting with great force before rejoining their circle. They then repeated the procedure. Another group pummelled the flailing headless neck, diverting its efforts to strike at Chuck until several of its plates were cracked and chipped.

After only a few minutes of this level of activity, W disengaged from Chuck and tried to retreat out of harm's way.

While this had been going on the V warrior was robbed of its moment of triumph by a volley of flying fighters smacking its head hard, involuntarily jerking it open and releasing Hadrian to tumble to the ground. His first lucky break was when his unconscious body landed in the leathery sac between the necks. This broke his fall and, as the Zapro had dropped towards the floor in reaction to the attack, Hadrian simply rolled off the sac onto the floor some half a metre below.

The warrior turned its attention to defending itself and was vigorously in the middle of its struggle when it noticed its colleague disengage and head off. Within a split second both damaged scouts were swimming away at great speed through the thin air doing the butterfly swim stroke as fast as their sacs would flap. Some Dugiri gave token chase and then returned to Pintar and the others.

Remarkably few Dugiri had been destroyed, but it meant that there was a little replacement haspira for Chuck. Hadrian was still knocked out.

Chuck got to his feet very painfully and checked out the damage. He prised the head away from his own and cast a concerned look at his thigh plates. Several were cracked and split, but the bite had not got through to his flesh. The leg and side which had been subjected to the lashing by the neck had also many cracked and loose plates but nothing that couldn't be repaired. He nodded to Pintar and one tile shook loose from high on his forehead, revealing a shock of white hair. He ignored it and crossed to Hadrian. Blood was trickling steadily from his head and the point where his neck met his shoulder. He propped him up against the wall and gathered some haspira to temporarily plug the flows. Hadrian had lost more blood than was comfortable. Chuck wished he had thought to make up a first aid kit. As he hadn't, he would have to return to his cave to mix his healing paste for Hadrian. He wasn't at all sure that Hadrian would last out that long. He lifted the boy's limp figure and turned in the direction of his cave.

*

CHAPTER 14

Pintar squirted over in front of Chuck's face and placed three fronds on the exposed hair on his brow. He heard a crackling sound in his forehead. Pintar added two more fronds and the crackling burst into a mentally transmitted communication.

"Dugiri mix will fix problem. Copernicus very near. Now Dugiri help Darkbeast."

There was no time to argue. Chuck just hoped the Dugiri mix would work. He nodded, turned and set off somewhat stiffly at first, after the swarm of allies. He soon extended his strides and ignored his own pain in his anxiety for Hadrian. At the back of his mind he wished they had managed to finish off the Zapro scouts once and for all. A Dugiri zapped beside him wearing Hadrian's catapult upside down. Perhaps it was simply carrying it in the only way it could but it looked very funny. Shortly after he noticed a mattress of Dugiri supporting his sword on the raft of their backs with their tendrils holding it steady. He was relieved to see that his sword had been lifted for him.

The journey did not take very long but it seemed like a lifetime because of the circumstances. On arriving at Copernicus, Hadrian was immediately laid on the leathery bed in the cave and medical preparations started. Several Dugiri started producing the sticky substance they oozed to repair their own cracks and splits. They dragged themselves slowly across Hadrian's neck or split head. The head wound was too deep for this gum to repair it but the neck showed slight improvement at its edges. Pintar pressed against Chuck's head and transmitted: 'Mix haspira, jellop, grow glop from nursery beds outside.' Chuck turned to see a group of Dugiri expressing jellop from their bodies onto a broken Zapro plate. Others flew in carefully balancing curved tiles of 'grow goo' on their backs. Three of them self-destructed next to Hadrian and left a clump of haspira behind.

Chuck cleared dust away from a small space on the cave floor. He made a nest of haspira, tipped the jellop onto it, then poured the glop over it. Working quickly, he mixed the concoction thoroughly until it became a lime green coloured paste. Cradling Hadrian's sleeping head in the crook of his arm, Chuck spread the mixture thickly over the neck slash until blood stopped seeping through it. How he wished he'd taken more time and made head armour for Hadrian. Regrets were not going to help the situation, so Chuck turned his attention to the deep head wound. Pinching its edges in, he smeared all of what was left of the mixture along the short length of the split. He sat in that position with one hand clamping the head wound until the mixture started to dry up and crumble. As flakes of the dry paste fell off the neck slash, Chuck and the silently suspended Dugiri looked on eagerly for some sign of life in Hadrian. There was none. Chuck wondered how much haspira Hadrian had taken. How much did he have in reserve? How much longer before it ran out and Hadrian stopped breathing altogether? The flakes of paste tumbled from Hadrian's neck until the wound was in full view. At least it would have been if it had still existed. Apart from a slight redness in the skin on the area previously cut, there was no evidence that there had ever been a slash there.

Some Dugiri did little somersaults and flips and a high-pitched humming sound from rubbing fronds filled the cold air of the cave.

Now for the head wound. Chuck had applied far more mixture to this wound, which was the more serious by far. He could already see that the paste had done a good job in reducing swelling and discolouration around the site. He still did not feel confident enough to release his finger clamp on the actual split. Gradually, surface flakes dried and broke free. There was still no reaction from Hadrian. Still Chuck held tight. The remaining paste was drying out more rapidly as it became less thick and soon the edges of the split could be seen .Chuck frowned. The cut was definitely still there. This job had been too much for the healing paste.

As the last bits dried up, Chuck carefully released the pressure of his finger clamp. As he did the wound opened to its original width. The only improvement was that it was very slightly reduced in width and length and had virtually stopped leaking blood.

This wasn't going to work. He laid Hadrian's head gently onto the leathery bed and thought of a desperate idea. Not knowing how much haspira Hadrian still had working away inside him didn't help at all. He looked up at Pintar and inclined his head in a gesture inviting the leader to come to him. Pintar understood and immediately approached and pressed several fronds against Chuck's hair.

He thought-transferred, "I'm very worried, Pintar. If I gave you directions to my cave could some of you go at superspeed and bring back some ingredients for me to try my healing paste?"

He felt the reply, 'Yes! Yes!'

Chuck leaned into Hadrian's armour and removed his map. He displayed it in front of Pintar who traced the exact route with one of his fronds. Chuck explained how to find his cave, access it, search out the petroleum jelly and scoop half a plate of it with a little fire sand into a small empty Zapro head. He then suggested they pluck half the head's capacity of haspira from his stash and add it to the other two ingredients in the makeshift bowl. This would start the mixing process as they brought it back to Copernicus, thus saving some precious time. Just before Pintar disengaged, Chuck asked, "I see you have some Zapro plates. Do you have any other bits? I could start a fire to warm Hadrian if I had certain bits."

"Pintar go now to Darkbeast cave. Two Dugiri show you Zapro remains. Back soon." Pintar disengaged, communicated with the others and immediately zoomed out into the earthlight followed by twenty flying colleagues. Two creatures flew up to Chuck's face and slowly retreated towards the cave opening giving occasional backflips. Chuck stood up and followed them outside where they led him to the destroyed form of SS93 behind the rocks. Eagerly, Chuck delved into the headless neck and grasped a handful of cables, wires, junctions and plastic wool and wrenched it clear. He repeated the procedure, getting an even bigger handful this time, some of it covered in an oily substance. He loped over to the separated head and plunged his hand deep into the cranium, ignoring the scraping of teeth and jaw blade on his armour plates. He wriggled his hand in deeper and deeper until he had a tight grip round a small cuboid. He yanked at it, like a dentist removing a stubborn tooth, until it broke free with a reluctant ripping sound. There were several short cables dangling from it and a red one in particular caused Chuck excitement. He went back to the rock, scooped up the entrails he had pulled out and headed back inside the cave.

Making a circular nest of innards topped with the oily ones, Chuck laid the cuboid on it like an egg and stroked the red cable over one corner of it. Sparks flew, startling some of the watching Dugiri. On the fourth attempt the sparks caught an oily cable sufficiently for a flame to leap into life. The flame ran along its cable and ignited a couple of others and the fire was established. The Dugiri were well back out of the way, but were watching with fascination at the scene in the corner. When the flames had a good hold, Chuck picked up his sword and went back outside. Naturally he was followed by a flock of inquisitive flying fruits. He smashed the head open with one mighty blow of the sword and used its tip to prise the main eye out. He repeated this for the two smaller ones and then took all three back to the fire. He placed the large one in the middle of the fire and retained the smaller two as fuel in reserve. The fire was causing some smoke to drift around the cave but the vast majority of it was sucked out of the cave opening along the ceiling. By the time the eye caught fire and quadrupled the heat level, Pintar's group were halfway to Chuck's cave.

Chuck stared down at Hadrian's figure. He had already suffered the loss of his two friends and was not about to let his new friend die. He added the other two eyes to the fire and the cave was bathed in a sleepy warmth. He fiddled with Hadrian's spear which some Dugiri had salvaged from Apollonius Crater. He turned it over in his hands, admiring the boy's handiwork. Most of the teeth had been snapped off in the battle. For wont of anything else to do, he stripped off the leather binding and shook free into the fire the broken remains of the teeth on the pole. The leathery fronds ignited on the healthy fire and he was left with the robot pole. Chuck couldn't believe it had come into his mind at that moment, but he decided there and then that if the worst happened, he would plant this rod at the head of Hadrian's grave and attach the bag of crystals to it. He had the picture in his mind as some of Pintar's party were scraping the petroleum-type jelly into the skull bowl while two others were shovelling a little fire dust in with it.

Chuck leaned back against the wall and became aware of his own aches and pains for the first time. He closed his eyes, felt the warmth of the cave surround him and dropped off into an immediate nap.

Chuck came to with a jolt. He bent over Hadrian and could still hear the vague sound of shallow breathing. He straightened up to the sound of Pintar and his party whooshing into the cave and hovering like a stacked tray. Pintar was at the bottom of the heap, three layers of Dugiri supported the weight of the filled skull and a double ring of the creatures flew in supporting formation round the middle of the skull, to keep it upright during the top-speed journey. It was scary the way they could zip into the cave then stop as one within a split second. Chuck nodded and reached up for the bowl. He squatted, cradling the skull between his tucked-up legs. He vigorously stirred and whirred the mixture until it started to thicken and turn a pale grey.

He then unintentionally astonished every Dugiri present by unclipping his left hand glove and then doing the same for his right. Their real surprise was when he worked at his head and unhooked the damaged armour to reveal a black human face with shining white long hair. He wanted to be ready to give artificial respiration if needed. Kneeling up, he cradled Hadrian in one arm and, with several Dugiri supporting the skull and just as many exploring his hair in utter fascination, he started to smear on the paste. As before, he finger-clamped the wound and worked the paste up and down the slit, across it and then rubbed some in a circular motion over the whole area. He sat back and waited. Pintar dropped some haspira near him. Chuck smiled and kept a tight hold on Hadrian's wound.

Pintar approached and lay some of his green communicating tendrils on Chuck's forehead.

"Darkbeast wear Zapro?"

"Yes, Pintar – for protection in battle. My real name is Chuck, not Darkbeast."

"Can Chuck mend Hadrian?"

"We've all done all we can. Now we must wait and hope."

The fire burned on and glowed against Hadrian's pale features. The paste started to crumble at the edges and fall to the floor. Chuck blew on Hadrian's head in a futile effort to dry the paste more quickly and had to force himself not to pick at the paste before it fell off itself. He pressed his cheek to Hadrian's nostrils. His breathing was faint and just beginning to sound laboured. Once or twice Chuck thought it had stopped altogether. He gently wiped dry paste from Hadrian's hair.

Another chunk broke off showing clear skin below. Just as Chuck was trying to remember if the split had been at that spot before, another dry lump dropped off where the split had been at its widest. There was no sign of any damage at all. Hadrian gave out a low groan. It was as if he had shouted out at his loudest. Chuck pulled him up a little, all the watching Dugiri dipped or swung slightly left and right as if in relief. Whether such a tense moment needed comic relief or not, it got it as a Dugiri pushed through to the front wearing Hadrian's catapult upside down, just as it had been carried all the way from the fight at Apollonius Crater. It looked totally silly, floating there like a space Teletubby. It was the first sight Hadrian saw when his eyes opened and his vision cleared and the force of his laughter shook the remainder of the dry healing paste from his head, revealing everything as good as new. Chuck prodded some haspira at his mouth which he wolfed down gladly. After four or five helpings he felt a lot better and sat up, looking at a beaming Chuck.

Pintar glided over and pressed four fronds against Chuck's forehead and two against Hadrian's scrambler, linking both humans in communication mode.

"Hey, welcome back buddy! Kinda thought we might have lost ya there!"

"I'm glad to be back. What happened?"

Chuck gave him details of the battle until he was knocked unconscious and Pintar took it up from that point. Hadrian was amazed at the thought of the Dugiri bringing the ingredients from Chuck's cave to theirs, "You're just like the flying doctors they have in Australia," he said, knowing that only Chuck would know what he meant.

He stood up a little groggily to find himself face to face with the catapulted Dugiri. He started to reach out to remove it then stopped.

"You keep it. It looks better on you than it does on me," he laughed. He dug behind his armour and placed his bag with the remainder of ball bearings down on the cave floor. "I'll leave you these in case you work out how to use it!" The Dugiri forward flipped twice by way of thank you, then zigzagged away as a bit of a celebrity by the way the others were frolicking with him.

Chuck replaced his head armour and Hadrian commented on the damage. Chuck just nodded and indicated all the cracked and chipped leg and body plates. He mimed stitching them all together again and gave a clap of his hands before covering them up too. He gathered up his sword and started munching a supply of haspira, obviously planning to leave now that Hadrian was safe with the Dugiri. Hadrian caught his glance.

"Please come back with me Chuck. I'll help you find your family if they are alive." He just shook his head, stepped forward and gave Hadrian a noisy hug and a thumbs up. Pintar transmitted, "Dugiri see Chuck soon," as Chuck gathered up his sword.

Waving to Pintar, he strode to the mouth of the cave and was gone from Hadrian's life.

Hadrian felt a huge lump in his throat and an equally huge lump in his pocket. The bag!

He started to unclip his armour from neck to waist. He slipped his arms out of the armour sleeves. They were somewhat damaged at the shoulders but not extensively. He released all the toggles holding his leg armour to his torso and stepped out of the leggings one at a time. Once out of his suit he was just about to heap it into a corner when an idea flew into his head. At first he dismissed it, then he saw his robot pole lying with no sharp teeth left on it and the idea took another step forward. When his eyes saw a certain piece of rock growing out of the wall within his reach, his mind was made up.

Mother Nature had fashioned this piece of solid rock so that it stuck out about 25cms from the wall at right angles to it and then turned sharply upwards at the end. It looked like a stone cloakroom peg. He threaded the robot pole through the shoulders of the suit of armour and checked it was tightly intertwined. Reaching up, he placed the metal pole over the rock hook at the neck of the jacket and pushed it towards the wall. The armour jacket dangled and swung to and fro as Hadrian toggled it up again. He was aware of a huge audience.

Bringing one leg over he fastened it to the torso and then repeated the procedure for the other leg. When he was finished he tweaked a tile here and a plate there, taking great care to finish up with the sleeves and legs hanging down like hollow circular tubes. He jumped up and dangled all his weight from the hook and it didn't even acknowledge his presence. 'Good,' he thought, this will work.

Taking a step back, he made sure the armour was swinging freely. It would be impossible for the suit to swing off the hook. The robot pole was a perfect support, the suit was hanging just as he wanted. He turned to Pintar and declared,

"Behold, my farewell present to my great friends!"

*

CHAPTER 15

"Hadrian Wall's Playsuit!"

He picked up a small rock and dropped it down one trouser leg, picked it up and repeated the exercise. He then held it in front of the other leg as if travelling upwards inside it and tried to make the whooshing sound that the Dugiri made when they flew. He passed the stone into the neck gap then dropped it down an arm, catching it at the bottom and then whooshing it down a leg. When it landed he stepped back and pointed to it calling out, "Dugiri! Dugiri!"

All at once the flying fruits seemed to realise what kind of playsuit this was and flew at it from all directions. They were having obvious great fun up the legs and down the legs, sometimes groups were travelling in both directions at once through the same tube and would somehow manage to pass each other with much clacking and shimmering of the plates, and zoom on. Like a swarm of bees in a busy hive they were going in and out in all directions and doing little flips of excitement when they emerged, only to plunge back in through some other opening. Despite the confined space and high speeds, there were no serious collisions, although now and then there would be the clack of a mid-air nudge or two.

Pintar's physique was such that he couldn't fit through the arm tubes, but he could manage the legs. Sometimes he would playfully hover to block access to an arm. He seemed to sense when to get out of the way just before a quiver of fruit arrows came shooting out of the sleeve from the opposite end. The Dugiri wearing the catapult flew towards an opening and hesitated, not sure if it could get through with its accessory. After a few seconds, two others helped it to lay the catapult flat along its back, wherein it immediately sped through the left leg. Hadrian grinned and still wondered about these little creatures who could obviously have fun, show compassion and communicate at a very advanced level. Yet they never felt pain nor acknowledged death. The next time he was in TESCO he was going to buy the dragon fruit which most resembled a Dugiri and coat it with matt varnish as an ornamental pet.

As he watched his pals enjoying themselves, he thought that this would be as good a time as any to take his leave. He crossed to the leathery bed and got out the crystals. He heard Pintar in his head.

"Grior's bag! Good this is that Hadrian has found, Dugiri thinks yes, is good."

He laid them all out on the bed, which attracted

some attention from inquisitive creatures. He couldn't remember getting his map out but there it was lying on the bed. He turned over his poster for his list of colours and sorted the crystals in order from the sun: Blue Mercury, Amber Venus, Crimson Mars, Purple Jupiter, Turquoise Saturn, Green Uranus, Yellow Neptune, Pink Pluto. He pulled out the remains of the clear Moonbiscuit crystal and the earth's bitten lime green one from his pockets. He also gathered together the travel pod capsules which were left. Everything seemed to be there, so Hadrian repacked it, retaining one travel capsule and the Earth crystal. The others he stuffed into his inside hoodie pocket. He walked out of the cave to gaze once more on planet Earth and to head for home. This had been an amazing adventure. Now to see what effects it has had at home. He stopped in the middle of the crater floor and turned to call farewell to Pintar. He jumped in surprise when he saw that what seemed like the entire Dugiri population had slipped out in total silence to wave him off. Pintar came forward;

"Special Dugiri farewell. Hadrian is Dugiri friend always!"

Spontaneously, the flying creatures swept into a kaleidoscope of colourful activities all around him. There were those moving in groups of five and seven as if being juggled by invisible hands. Others were performing synchronised movements, 'Red Arrows'-type formation flypasts, high speed criss-cross flying from groups passing through each other's formations without any clashes, Ten Dugiri stacked vertically flew past with the catapult creature on top. There were several other flips, flops, circles and spins in a fantastic blitz of action. Hadrian waved expansively, fighting his emotions so much that he decided to leave right away before he embarrassed himself. He looked at the tasteless guava juice look-alike and bit the capsule. It dissolved in an instant. Hadrian took the Earth crystal and bit it as a Cadbury's crème egg. The delicious taste of chocolate and fondant filled his mouth and nose as he spun away from his lunar farewell towards an Earthly welcome.

On his outward journey he had experienced images of several moons but on the return leg he had a jumble of odd mini-nightmares. He saw a scene of a Zapro warrior killing Chuck. The astronaut then exploded and thousands of tiny Zapro came scuttling out of his body. Suddenly, Hadrian's feet were there and the tiny monsters started nibbling his toes. He tried to kick out at his attackers but his legs wouldn't move. This scene faded into one where Dugiri were appearing through his bedroom ceiling and splatting themselves on the carpet. His mother was running around with the Dyson shouting, "You and your spacemen," as she vacuumed them up. The Dyson machine was bulging fit to explode. His third vision was of his father and mother each having a lower torso like Grior's, ending in a ball. They were zooming around in circles in the garden collecting pebbles which they were lobbing into

Hadrian's mouth. He was sitting up in his flying saucer pram. The fourth was simply an awful scene of Spangles ripping Grior to shreds while Lorna hummed 'God Save The Queen'. They all mixed in and out with each other, merging and fading at random. Hadrian could do nothing to turn these off although he knew they weren't real.

His back was drenched with sweat and large beads of perspiration dripped from his hair. He was relieved when they all faded and planet Earth swam into view. He could see the continent of Africa stretched out below him. His capsule was maintaining a course from South Africa to Gibraltar. As he neared earth it swung up through Germany to Latvia, turning abruptly towards the UK. The capsule gathered speed and dropped towards Earth's atmosphere like a rocket. Suddenly there was a massive shunt and shudder as they entered and Hadrian blacked out.

He was aware he was spinning fiercely. He stopped suddenly without any discomfort and the travel pod disintegrated into vapour in the blink of an eye. He was home! Hadrian slowly looked round his bedroom. The bed was made just as he had left it and everything else seemed to be in place. Where was Grior? The clock showed ten minutes to eight, which would normally mean that it must be the weekend. On schooldays his mum would have been in at seven-thirty for first call. At the weekend she would come in at eight. He crossed to the window where the signs of life below confirmed it was morning. A Paper Girl was doing her rounds and bottles of milk were on the doorsteps of a few houses. He sat on the edge of his bed and tried to transmit to Grior that he was home. The note to his parents was still stuck to his laptop frame. It must be Saturday! He had only been gone overnight. He stood up to go and remove his note when the wind suddenly penetrated the window and billowed the curtains, stopping him in his tracks. A few seconds later, Grior and he were standing facing each other beside the bed

"Grior!" Hadrian whispered as loudly as he dared. He stretched his arms out and touched his friend on the shoulder areas. Grior made noises of delight and partially wrapped his extendable arm round Hadrian's back, coaxing him gently into a hug.

"Welcome back, Hadrian. I am so relieved you have returned safely. I was worried all night."

"All night? So all of this has just lasted one night right enough?"

"Yes and no Hadrian. Just before you left I implanted a time compressor in your shoulder. It should self-disintegrate within a day or so. You will feel just a little sharp jab."

"A time compressor? Explain to me Grior!"

"It is a device we can use if we are leaving one planet's time to do something in a different time sector. I set yours for ten hours.

I implanted it into your shoulder when you were leaving for the moon."

"I *felt* a sharp nip but thought you had done it accidentally."

"I'm afraid I didn't tell you about it because I didn't think it would work on you. You have only used eight hours so expect a jaggy pain in two hours' time in your left shoulder. But you haven't told me yet, did you get the Universe Crystals, Hadrian? Can I get home?"

Hadrian grinned and teasingly pulled out the bag very slowly. Grior swivelled repeatedly in excitement while Hadrian chuckled quietly. He laid the bag on his bed and tipped out the contents. Grior immediately snatched up the purple one and lifted a travel capsule too.

"All that I need to get home! Thank thank thank you Hadrian!"

"The rest of it all seems to be here, too" said Hadrian as he dropped the crystals one by one into the Bag, followed by the remaining travel capsules. "Could I have a chunk of your Jupiter crystal as a souvenir, Grior?" he ventured.

"A piece of this crystal – *and* a travel pod to come and visit me. In fact, two travel pods and the rest of the Earth crystal too, in case you come to visit me and somehow it doesn't work. At least you'll be able to get safely home."

Grior snapped off a piece of purple crystal with his pincer hand and gave it over to Hadrian.

"Did you have much trouble getting the Universe Bag back?"

"Apart from fighting Zapro three times, trekking over the moon, befriending flying fruit, meeting two monsters that were really one, only to find out it was something else altogether and being knocked out, do you mean? Nah, it was easy, especially the underground swimming!"

Hadrian fished out the remaining chunk of lime green crystal from the bag, "Thanks very much, Grior. I don't know when, but I am determined to visit you some day."

"Wait a moment. I have my crystal and travel pod organised. Why don't you keep the Universe Bag as a reward for all you went through to get it. I can get other crystals back home, although I won't be going anywhere for a while! You deserve this at least for your courage and friendship."

Hadrian's eyes were like huge flying saucers.

"Wow, that would be brilliant, Grior." He stood up and rifled through his pockets for some kind of souvenir for Grior. He threw his hoodie over a chair then dug into his jeans.

"This is all I've left for you, Grior. It's the map showing my journeys on the moon. I've given away my knife and catapult, it's all I've left."

Grior took the map and stored it in the appropriate slit in his chest. "This map will be a wonderful reminder."

There was a finality in Grior's tone and Hadrian knew he was about to head away. The next thirty seconds passed in a flash. Mum could be heard singing as she approached Hadrian's room. Hadrian pushed the bag under his duvet. Grior took the capsule and threw the crystal into his flap. He and Hadrian exchanged glances which said more than could ever be described in print. Grior spun as the door handle turned and mum entered the room, switching the light on.

"Oh, you're up? Well seen it's Saturday!" she exclaimed as she crossed over towards the window. Her attention was drawn to the note on the computer. "Jogging? You? Before breakfast? There's something odd about this, Hadrian Wall."

"I'm not long back. I just couldn't sleep."

"When you can't sleep you play with your PlayStation, you never go jogging!" His mother had reached the curtains and pulled them open. Down below she saw Lorna closing her gate as she returned home from walking the dog. She glanced up and gave Mrs Wall a wave and a smile. Mrs. Wall beamed back. "Jogging indeed!" Hadrian's mum stood at the window adding two and two together and getting five. "Mind you, if you've decided jogging's better, then I'm all for it!" she said turning to face Hadrian. He was more than a little bemused by his mother's change of tone.

"What happened to your jeans!?" she demanded, noticing the split.

"Oh, I-I forgot to tell you about that. It happened at Robbie's the other day. I was messing about with Robbie and Spangles and I caught them on something.

Sorry, Mum, I meant to tell you."

'Messing about with Robbie indeed,' she thought, 'More likely showing off in front of Lorna.'

"Leave them out for the wash and I'll see if anything can be done. In fact, if you've been out *jogging* leave your jeans, hoodie, and stuff on the landing and I'll put them in the wash. Now, come on – up, your pals will be here at nine and you've still to shower, dress and have breakfast." As she switched off the light on the way out, she shouted, "And don't forget to pull your duvet off the bed so I can change it while you're at the football!"

As soon as she left the room Hadrian ran to the window. He concentrated on his language scrambler, "Goodbye, Grior, have a safe journey home."

For a few seconds there was silence then, very 'grainy,' the reply came, 'Bye, Hedrnnn. Zangk yoooo....' The message faded and he felt a popping in his ears. The scrambler had expired.

Hadrian pulled off his jeans and socks, T-shirt and boxers. He stuck his head round the door and dropped the heap of washing against the wall. He fetched a robe from the wardrobe and made for the shower. His dad was just emerging from the loo.

"Morning Beckham! Who are we going to slaughter today? Brazil? A Combined European Star Select? A World Eleven?"

"Elmbank Primary, in the Cup," replied Hadrian.

"A sell-out for sure, ticket touts crowding the

playground, mounted police controlling the fans."

The last thing Hadrian heard before he turned on the shower was, "Give you a quid for every goal you score; score none and you wash the car."

"You're on!" replied Hadrian and proceeded to shower the moon dust off his face and out of his hair. He was drying himself when his mum's voice split the silence.

"Hadrian! What's this muck in your pocket!?"

Without even thinking, he replied, "Sorry, it's haspira, mum!" As soon as he said it he regretted it. If he had to explain haspira, he had a lot of explaining to do.

In the kitchen, the reply Jill heard was, "Sorry, it was Peter, Mum!"

She responded, "It was Peter was it?! Well you tell him from me that if he stuffs muck into your pockets again his mother will get the bill for the cleaning!" Whoever Peter was, she wondered.

When Hadrian heard his mum's reply he went into silent convulsions of laughter. It was part relief and part utter pleasure at the ridiculously funny miscommunication. He returned to the bedroom and dressed. He pulled back the duvet as he had been told and there lay the Universe bag. Hadrian had forgotten he'd stuffed it away in the panic caused by his mum's eight o'clock visit. He sat on the bed and ran the bag over both palms, admiring the beautiful contents. Should he tell his parents?

"Breakfast!"

"OK."

Probably not, but he had an idea. He carefully placed the bag at the back of his secrets drawer and went down to breakfast. He could only face Weetabix and a small banana when he was going to play football. While eating it, his dad said, "I hear you were jogging first thing, son. You must be awfully worried about Elmbank."

Tony and Jill exchanged secret smirks.

"I just couldn't sleep. Dad, you know how you write articles? Well this blind black man was waiting at the taxi rank today. He had dropped his glove and I stopped to give it to him. He asked why I was out of breath and we started chatting. He said he was going back to the USA to die. He seemed sad. I told him you wrote for magazines and he said, 'For your kindness I will tell you a true story'. He said his name was Myles and that in 1964 his dad 'Chuck' Giemza was sent on a secret Apollo SH mission to land on the moon, with two other astronauts, Popeye Kennedy and Jake Early. They were all lost and the government has never admitted that the mission happened."

"What nonsense! Tony Wall, this is your doing! He's getting as airy-fairy as you!" exclaimed Jill. "Here come the boys, off you go the pair of you."

Dad looked at Hadrian in a way he had never looked at him before and started to jot down the names Hadrian had just given him.

About an hour later, Robbie sprinted down the left wing and crossed a beautiful ball into the box where Hadrian rose and headed his second and his team's third goal, for a 3 – 0 lead. As he turned to celebrate he felt a sharp jab in his shoulder as the time compressor imploded.

Lorna was cheering and applauding him. Hadrian was happy.